CAPTIVATED

Is é an grá an rud ar fad.
Níl ionainn ach píosaí.

CARFANO CRIME FAMILY
BOOK 6

REBECCA GANNON

newsletter, contact me, blog, shop, and links to all social medias: www.rebeccagannon.com

More by Rebecca Gannon

Pine Cove
Her Maine Attraction
Her Maine Reaction
Her Maine Risk
Her Maine Distraction

Carfano Crime Family
Casino King
The Boss
Vengeance
Executioner
Wild Ace
Captivated

Standalone Novels
Whiskey & Wine
Redeeming His Reputation

*To the stubborn, hyper-independent girls
who secretly want the princess treatment,
this is for you.*

THE CARFANO FAMILY

Leo (d)
(m) Katarina (d)

Michael (d)	Salvatore (d)	Anthony	Richard	Maria
(m) Anita	(m) Teresa	(m) Francesca	(m) Christina	(m) Carmine
Leo, Alec, Luca, Katarina	Nico, Vincenzo, Mia	Stefano, Marco, Gabriel	Saverio, Gia, Aria	Matteo, Elena

(m) – married / (d) – deceased

"I never expected you to get under my skin,
but now your name runs through my veins
and I can't help but let every
part of you in."

- Courtney Peppernell
"Pillow Thoughts"

CHAPTER 1

Cassie

I keep my eyes cast downward, but that doesn't mean I can't feel every pair of eyes in here pass over me.

Be brave, Cass. You've got this.

This is the only way you know how to help Sean, and you're going to fucking do it.

I lift my eyes and quickly scan the room, seeing nothing but beautiful girls, all at various stages of doing their hair, makeup, and getting dressed.

Well, I use *dressed* as a relative term, considering what's being put on covers less than what they had on to begin with.

"Hey, Newbie," the striking brunette who's applying eyeliner at one of the vanities greets, then meets my eyes in the mirror. "I'm Kay."

"Hi." I clear my throat. "Cassie."

"You can use this station," she says, pointing to the vanity next to her. "Kendra isn't working tonight."

"Thanks." I place my duffel bag down on the floor and pull out my makeup bag, taking a deep breath while I stare at my blank reflection in the mirror.

"Nervous?" Kay asks after a moment.

"A little."

"First time?"

"Yeah. I've been taking classes for fun for the past few years, but…" I trail off, glancing over at her.

"You never thought you'd be doing it for money?"

I huff out a short laugh. "Something like that."

"We all have a story, honey. We all have something that brought us here. Good or bad." I nod in agreement. How spot on she is. "Can I give you some advice?"

"Sure."

"When you solve whatever problem brought you here, quit."

"I plan to."

"It's not always that easy," she says with a distant look to her eyes. Then, coming to her senses, her eyes clear and she studies me. "Do you have a stage name yet? Or an act?"

"An act?"

"Yeah. A persona you can slip into. It helps keep distance between you and them. You don't want them knowing your real name."

I pause to think, and Kay smiles. "I have something for you if you don't know yet." She walks over to her locker and shuffles a few things around on the top shelf before grabbing something in the back. "I bought this a few months ago thinking I was going to change things up, but it didn't work for me. For you, though, I think it will. Especially with that gorgeous red hair."

Kay holds up a lace mask with cat ears and I can't help but smile. It will match what I'm going to wear perfectly while also covering the top half of my face.

"What are you wearing?" she asks me, and I bring my bag to my lap. I pull out a pair of black lace cheeky bottoms, along with a matching black lace corset top. "Good. It matches. You can be the sexy little red-haired kitten all the men wish they had purring in their laps." She winks, sitting back down at her vanity.

I scoff. "I won't be purring in anyone's lap."

"Unless they want a lap dance. But another piece of advice… Don't mix business and pleasure. These men will see you as their fantasy, but outside of these walls," she pauses, lining her bottom lip with red lip liner, "that fantasy bubble bursts. I made that rookie mistake when I first started dancing, and I learned the hard way that these men think we'll do anything for a few bucks. Even when we're not clocked in. And when you don't act like their fantasy, they'll show you what they really think of you."

I swallow hard and clear my throat. "I'm sorry."

"It's okay, honey. I was naïve then. I danced my way out of that naivety real quick." With a little smirk, Kay finishes lining her lips and then glides a matching red lipstick across her lips. "I can already tell you're not as naïve as I was. But I'm here if you need anything. We all are. This isn't a caddy place where we're all out for our own gain. We look out for one another."

"Thank you. I appreciate that."

I go behind the room divider curtains and change into my stage outfit, and when I emerge, Kay leans back in her chair and looks me up and down with a wide grin.

"You were hiding a killer body under those sweats, girl."

"Thanks, I guess." I laugh, and sit back down to finish my makeup. I had my base face makeup done, but not my eyes or lips.

When I came in for the job, the manager told me the main stage is where girls make the most money, but they have to earn their place there. I told him I was more comfortable as a side stage dancer anyhow.

On the side stages, I'm able to do my own thing. No one can get close enough to touch me, and I don't need to take anything off unless I want to. Even if I did take my clothes off to get more tips, this is a titties-only club, which was why I chose it over the others in town. I don't want to be forced to show more than I'm willing to or am comfortable with.

If I'm being honest, I don't even want to show my boobs to a room full of strangers, let alone my entire ass and pussy. I'm confident, but not that confident.

For the women who do go full nude, I admire their confidence. Plus, the power they must feel when they have every set of eyes in the club on them must be like nothing else. Admired and desired, yet still untouchable and unattainable.

When I'm finished with my makeup and hair, I stand in front of the mirror. Noticing the slight tremor in my hands, I fist them at my sides and take a deep breath, remembering why I'm doing this.

Just pretend I'm in the studio and having fun.

No one will recognize me.

No one will touch me.

I grab the mask Kay gave me and tie it around my head. I pull out the top layer of my hair and pin the ribbon in place to hide it in my hair and keep it in place.

"I knew it'd look good on you." Kay gives me a smile and a wink. "Have fun out there, Cassie. Men are easy."

A laugh I didn't expect bubbles out of me at that statement. "That they are."

"Kay, you're up in 5 minutes," the house mom says. "Cassie, you're going out there with Jaylan in 5, too."

I look around to see who Jaylan is, and Kay points to a girl curling her hair across the room.

"That's Jay. She'll be up on the other satellite stage while I'm on the main stage. After I'm done, you'll stay there for the next two girls while they're on the main stage as well."

"Alright."

"Just vibe to the music and do whatever you want, basically."

"Got it."

I'm nervous, but also a little excited now. I barely recognize myself in the mirror, and it helps with my nerves.

I've fucking got this.

I'm the bitch who does what she wants.

I'm the bitch who knows she can get whatever she wants.

I'm the bitch who can conquer the damn world if I so well please.

Turing so I can see my reflection from all angles, the sparkles imbedded in my nude fishnet tights twinkle, and I do I few stretches before I slip my feet into my black pleaser heels. Once they're secured around my ankles, I do a few more stretches and meet Jaylan and Kay by the door.

Jaylan gives me an encouraging smile. "Just look to me if you freeze or need inspiration, okay? I've been doing this a while."

"Okay." I nod, taking another deep breath.

The music had been a dull thumping beat in the background while in the dressing room, but once we leave, it starts to pulse through my veins and my hips automatically sway with every step down the hallway and out onto the main floor.

Kay walks down into the VIP pit area and steps up onto the stage while Jaylan and I separate and walk on either side of the club to our satellite stages. A security guard holds his hand out for me to take and he helps me up the hidden stairs to my platform.

There's a pole in one corner to use for balance and as a prop rather than for a full performance, as well as a waist-high railing around the platform to grab onto.

My eyes sweep the club, taking in every pair on me, feeling even the ones from the shadows. I want to hate it, like I'm doing something wrong, but that's not it at all. I don't hate it. I feel sexy and desired.

I just can't think about what they're thinking.

I can't think about how they see me.

I can't think about anything.

I close my eyes for a moment and let my body feel the music and move however it wants.

I open my eyes again and they lock with a man sitting three tables away. I run my hands out along the railing, bending forward. The songs blend together and I make sure I lock eyes with different men every minute to keep them on me.

As Kay said…men are easy.

Each one makes their way to me and I snake my hips down to their level so some can slip money into the waist of my bottoms, while with others, I take it from their hands and slip it between my breasts while giving them a little wink.

Again, men are easy.

When my songs are up, the security guard helps me down, and I saunter back to the dressing room. A huge smile spreads across my face when I see Kay.

"I'm guessing you had fun?" she asks.

"I did. It was like taking candy from grown babies."

"Exactly." She smirks.

"Cassie, you were great," Stella, the house mom, says. "You three are up again in twenty."

Taking the money out of my waistband and top, I shove it into the zipper pouch I brought with me and Kay does the same. "If you ever make it up to the main stage, the money thrown at your feet will be swept up and brought to you, along with whatever clothing you take off."

"Good to know. Thanks."

I touch up my makeup and hair, drink some water, and when it's our time again, I take Jaylan's stage while she goes to the main stage, and Kay takes the stage I was on.

There are more people in here now, but with a deep breath, I once again let the music pulse through me and let the beat move my body.

CHAPTER 2
Nico

This meeting needs to fucking end.

I need to get back to the city. Being in this town, in the same one as *her*, is making me itch with the need to find her. To touch her soft skin and run my fingers through her hair.

Fuck…

I shift in my chair and rub my jaw.

Images fill my mind of me wrapping her silken rope of fire around my fist and yanking her head back so I can hear her moan as I kiss her neck and she rides my dick.

Fuck me.

I wipe my hands down my face and keep my expression neutral.

She's the best I've ever had. No competition. No comparison.

Three days with her wasn't enough. I agreed to her terms of no-strings-attached fun for a weekend while I was visiting my brother in January, thinking I'd have no problem going back to New York and back to reality. But Cassandra fucking Connelly has snuck into my thoughts every chance she could.

Time hasn't lessened her presence in my mind. It's been over a month and I can still hear her soft moans and mewls for more when I close my eyes at night from when I woke her in the early morning with my tongue sliding through her pussy. But it's not even just my waking thoughts. She haunts my fucking dreams, too, and I wake up with my hand around my cock, aching for her.

Jesus, Nico, get a fucking grip.

She's busy with school. Plus, I doubt she's as delusional as I am and stuck on me like I am her.

I reach for the bottle of water in front of me and gulp down half of it, trying to calm the fire in me before I go fucking crazy.

Yeah, too fucking late.

"If no one has anything else they want to discuss?" Leo asks, letting his words hang in the air for a few seconds before nodding and pushing his chair away from the table.

Thank fucking God.

We moved our monthly meeting to Atlantic City this month instead of holding it in our Manhattan office like usual. With Tessa being pregnant, Alec can't be away from her for even a day. We learned that the hard way last month when he found out she wasn't feeling well during our meeting and went off on us for being so far from her when she needed him.

Alec before Tessa was an asshole. Alec after Tessa was a tolerable asshole. But Alec with a pregnant Tessa? He's a crazy motherfucker who's taken his overprotective ass to a new level of crazy. Which is why this month, we're meeting in Atlantic City at our family's casino, The Aces, so that he's close to Tessa if she needs him.

Being here is fucking with my head, though.

I met Cassandra in our club, Royals, here at The Aces.

I told myself to stay away from her. Nothing good can come to her life with me in it aside from amazing fucking sex, and I'm not fucking up the good shit she has going for her by asking her for more of anything.

"Vin, you want to grab something to eat?" I ask my brother, which has Saverio and Matteo, our cousins who run our Miami club, turning back as they're leaving.

"Were you not going to invite us?" Sav asks sarcastically.

"You're the one walking out the door."

"Because you've had a pissed-off look on your face this entire meeting."

"And?" I question.

"And I thought that was a sign to tell us all to leave you alone."

"I'm fine," I clip.

Sav raises his eyebrows, knowing I'm lying. "Okay."

Vinny slaps my back and grips my shoulder. "Let's get some food."

The four of us, plus Gabriel, Marco, and Stefano, go to dinner while Alec goes back to Tessa, Leo to Abri, and Luca to Angela. I'm surprised Vinny doesn't say he needs to get home to Lexi, but I'm not going to question it. Mostly because I think his answer would involve pitying me somehow, and I don't want his fucking pity.

Vinny had a front row seat to Cassie and I meeting. It was the night he met Lexi, too. I never told him I spent the weekend with Cassie, but I'm sure Lexi told him. He knew she was something to me when he asked me for her number when Lexi was in trouble, but he knows better than to ask me about her or I'll kick his ass.

I didn't understand the instant obsession and need my cousins had when they met their women, but I do now. Cassandra fucking Connelly has had me captivated from the moment she locked eyes with me and told me to dance with her. There was absolutely no hesitation on my part. I pulled her close and let her rock her sexy ass against me, driving me so wild, I was about ready to drag her to a dark corner and slide my hand up under her short little dress to see if she was as affected as I was.

I found out just how much she was later that night.

And all weekend.

She's beautiful, confident, sexy, freaky, and got under my skin unlike any woman I've ever met or been with.

I shake my head and free myself from the vivid memories that still haunt me, and try and stay present at dinner.

When we're done eating, Stef says he's going back to the hotel to work on something, but my other cousins aren't ready to let the night end like I wish it would.

"Let's hit up the club or something," Sav says. "I know you have Lexi, Vin, but you can be our wingman."

"Nope," he says quickly, shaking his head and smiling. "You don't need me to pick up women, and my girl's waiting for me."

"Yeah, yeah, yeah. While you're with Lexi, we'll be getting lap dances from the city's finest. They're not Miami girls, but I know our family only employs the most beautiful girls in their clubs."

"That we do," Vinny says, and gives everyone handshakes and one-armed hugs. "See you next month. Try to keep this one out of trouble tonight." Vin nods towards me and I return his snarky grin with a glare of my own.

"Don't worry. We'll get him a dance and he'll cheer right up," Matteo says.

"Pussy tends to do that," Marco adds with a crooked grin.

"And with that, I have to go." Vinny laughs, backing away with his hands up before turning on his heel and walking quickly to his car.

"There isn't one woman on this planet that could make me want to run home to her. The same pussy every night? It'd have to be magic and casting a spell on me for that to happen."

"Matty, I'll warn you once," I tell him, looking him straight-on so I know he hears me. "Don't ever say that in front of any of them. You'll end up with a hole in you that wasn't there before."

Matteo shrugs with a shit-eating grin. "I'll take that under advisement. Now, let's go." He rubs his hands together.

The drive to Dark Horse, our family's strip club here in Atlantic City, isn't too far. When we park, I look at the building and the red neon sign that used to signal a good night for me.

I'm not really in the mood for this, but who knows, maybe there will be a girl who will help me get over my obsession with a certain spicy redhead.

The layout of the club was carefully planned out so that right from the moment a person opens the door, they're taken away from the reality of the outside world and immersed in another.

The bouncers give us nods of acknowledgement and open the doors for us without saying a word.

It's dark, with red and purple lighting. Black leather wallpaper covers the walls for a textured, luxurious look and feel, and black carpet mutes our steps. The club's music is pumped in low and subdued with high bass, until you reach the end where another bouncer pulls a curtain back to let us through.

Sam, the club's manager, spots us and walks right up to me. "Good evening, Mr. Carfano. We have your table for you down in the pit and I'll have a waitress sent right over to you."

"Thanks, Sam." He nods and walks over to talk with one of the bartenders and a waitress while we walk deeper into the club.

At the entrance to the VIP pit area where we'll be eye-level with the dancers on the stage, a security member removes the velvet rope for us. The others take the three steps down first, and just as I'm about to, my eyes sweep the room in front of me, stopping when I catch a flash of red that's all too familiar.

My hands fist at my sides and my eyes run down every inch of her. Her back is to me, but I know it's her.

I can see the tattoo I traced and memorized with my tongue on the back of her upper left thigh. And I know if those tiny little panties showed the top of her ass cheeks rather than the bottom half, then I'd see the little shamrock tattoo she has above her right one.

I spent three days memorizing every inch of her body, and now it's on display for these filthy fucking assholes who are no doubt imagining everything they could do with her. But they won't. Over my dead fucking body will anyone get to do what I've already done and want to do again. And again. And fucking again.

I know all too well what her body is capable of because she's made me use my hand more than I ever have in my goddamn life, trying to get her out of my head.

But only she will do.

No other woman. No other pussy. No other ass. No other anything.

Dammit.

Why the fuck is she here? How long has she been working here?

No.

Fuck no.

I don't want anyone else to see or know how her body moves. Especially against them if she's asks to give a private dance.

I can't fucking see straight.

The lights in here are messing with my vision and all I see is red.

What the fuck is happening to me?

I'm the calm one. I'm the voice of reason in the family when decisions need to be made. But right now, I'm anything but calm. I could kill everyone in here for just looking at her. And I'm about to if I don't do something.

Cassie tosses her hair around and rolls her body like the little tease she is. She drops down low, swirls her hips, and whips her head and body around to the front – finally letting me see her beautiful face.

Fuck. Me.

Her beauty punches me in my gut.

Her eyes sweep the tables in front of her, but like she can feel my gaze, her eyes lift and lock with mine.

Cassie freezes, gripping the railing in front of her as she takes me in from head to toe and back like she's checking to see if it's really me. Her eyes widen when she realizes it is.

"Get everyone out of here," I tell the security guy still waiting for me to move.

"Excuse me, Mr. Carfano?"

"I said," I grit out, "get everyone out of here. Now." My voice is the only part of me that's calm in any sense. "Everyone but her." I lift my chin to Cassie, and I see the bouncer out of the corner of my eye press the button on the cord of his ear piece as he relays my message.

My eyes never leave Cassie's.

She's about to know the mistake she made.

CHAPTER 3
Cassie

With my back to the club, I roll my neck and reach up, grabbing the pole in front of me. I stretch up and arch my back like a cat, then slowly weave my hips from side to side while moving down into a squatted position. Swirling my hips, I pop back up with my ass in the air and then spin around, slowly sliding up the pole until I'm fully standing.

I raise my eyes to find my first victim of this stage set's seduction, and instead, am met with a pair I've already fallen victim to.

I grip the railing in front of me – frozen.

He's here.

Why is he here?

He's staring right back at me, and I know he knows it's me with the thundering look of anger covering his handsome face. This mask isn't fooling him.

Nico Carfano.

The man that blew my goddamn mind and back out for three days straight. The man that had me seeing stars. The man that left my throat raw from how many times he had me screaming. The man that gave me everything and nothing at the same time, with no promises for anything past the weekend.

We had a no-strings-attached deal, and we both honored that.

Then why is he looking at me like that? And why is my heart beating double-time and my stomach knotting up at him seeing me like this?

Nico's lips move as he says something to the security guard beside him. His face only grows angrier, and he says something again.

I haven't moved an inch and his eyes haven't left mine.

The manager of the club joins them and Nico says something to him that has the man wide-eyed and rubbing the back of his neck. But he nods and starts talking into his earpiece.

The security guard that was by my stage moves away and starts going around to every table, urging those sitting to stand and leave.

I look back to Nico and see he's watching everything I do, and the corner of his mouth tilts up in a devilish little smirk that has my stomach knotting further.

What is he doing?

The music cuts off, and as the club slowly empties, a few of the customers put up a drunken fuss, but security has no problem pushing them out the door.

Four men are beside Nico now, and they look over to me before quickly looking away when Nico says something harsh in reply. I can see it in the set of his mouth.

Oh, that mouth of his. I know it has the capability of saying and doing the dirtiest things, and right now, seeing him use it to command people to do what he wants… It has my pussy throbbing at the memory of him commanding me to get on my knees, to get on my stomach, my back, on the counter, against the windows, the tiles of the shower, and everywhere in between.

Fuck.

My knees shake and my elbows buckle as I lean forward so I don't collapse to the floor in a puddle of need.

I don't let men affect me like this. I use them for what I need and then I'm done. I don't get attached unless I want to. Before that weekend I spent with Nico, of course.

I followed the rules we made.

I kept it at three days of fun.

I knew he was going back to his life in New York City and I was staying here in Atlantic City to finish my last semester of college.

He's made studying quite difficult, though. Every time I had to focus on what the professor was saying or what I was reading, I'd hear or see a word that had my mind connecting it to Nico, and then I'd be lost in my head for a while until I realized what I was doing and snapped out of it.

One weekend with him, learning every inch of each other's bodies and what drives the other absolutely crazy, and I've been ruined. That was all it was meant to be, though. That's all it was – carnal fucking lust.

At least, I thought so.

The music is turned off and the club empties, allowing me to hear my heart pounding wildly in my chest.

He's going to hear it. He's going to know.

The manager comes back and says something else to Nico, who nods and replies, which has the manager quickly ushering out all the employees, too.

Before I can think of what I should do, and before I can get my legs to work properly to find my way out too, we're alone in the club.

Just Nico and I.

Just us in this big empty club.

Alone.

"Were you hoping no one would recognize you with that mask?" he asks, taking the three steps down into the VIP pit area. I nod, and he pulls a chair from one of the tables and turns it so it's directly in front of the main stage. "You want to dance? Come and dance for me, Cassandra."

His tone leaves no room for argument, and apparently all my body needed was for him to say my name and command me to do something in order for me to be able to finally move.

I step down from the stage and walk over to the set of stairs across from him. His eyes follow my every move. They're like two dark flames burning every inch of my skin exposed to him – making his mark.

He's tattooing me with his gaze.

I still remember the feeling of him tracing my tattoos. With his fingers first, and then his tongue. He loved them. And now he's giving me his own tattoo that's adorning me in invisible ink of his own pattern.

With it being just us here, my usual confidence steadily comes back to me with every step until I'm the girl I was with him that weekend. The girl who saw what she wanted and took it without shame.

It was the most intense experience of my life.

I knew with his brother dating my best friend, I'd maybe eventually see him again. I didn't think it'd be so soon, and especially not here, like this.

Nico pulls out his phone and dials a number. "Is everyone gone? Did you leave yet? … Turn the music back on and then leave. Lock the door behind you."

He slips his phone back into his pocket and leans back in the chair, spreading his legs. Those long, muscular legs I already know I fit perfectly between while on my knees.

The music turns back on, and Nico rubs his bottom lip with his thumb. "Dance for me, Red."

His deep voice vibrates through me and settles in my core while his eyes take me in from head to toe and back. He has a full, unobstructed view of me now that I'm front and center before him.

Red.

He called me that in the club when we first met. We were dancing, and with his arms snaked around me, he tugged on the ends of my hair and whispered in my ear, "Come up to VIP with me, Red. Let me see if you're just as fiery off the dance floor."

My God, I was so fucking turned on. Everything he did and said that night had me in a hazy trance that made me want more and more.

I still want more.

"Closer" by Nine Inch Nails starts playing through the sound system, and I feel the music like it's a part of my blood. A part of my heartbeat.

Each hit of the beat has me loosening and becoming the Cassie I was with him.

I can be her again.

I can show him everything I know and be the girl who captivates his attention from the stage.

I want his eyes on me.

I want to feel them watching me while I seduce him and he can't touch me while I do so.

Licking my lips, I wait for the first line of the song to begin, and I walk around the pole. On the next line, I slither my hips from side to side, moving down the pole as I go. I circle my hips and thrust them forward twice when he sings, "*I want to penetrate you.*"

Nico shifts in his seat and I slide back up the pole, rolling my head and tossing my curls around.

On the first, "*help me*," I circle the pole, lift myself up, and do a corkscrew spin, loving the feeling of being off the ground. On the next, I flip over into a spinning chopper. And on the third one, I hook my leg around the pole and spin down into a hand stand and spread my legs into a split.

Bending one knee, I swing down to my knees with my back to Nico and pop up onto my toes – legs spread and bent forward.

As the chorus approaches, I grip the pole and swing backwards, dropping to the floor on my knees again as he sings, "*I want to fuck you like an animal.*"

I slide my arms forward with my ass in the air and circle my hips before spreading my knees apart and thumping my hips against the stage twice.

Arching my back, I stretch my hands out all the way in front of me and lift my feet in the air, circling them, and slowly sliding down to the floor until I'm lying flat. And when the same line repeats, I make my legs like a number four and hump the floor twice before swinging my leg around so I'm in a split.

I grab the pole and lift myself up, sliding my toes together until I'm standing. And when the song says, "*closer to God,*" I jump onto the pole and swing around in a split and then flip upside down and twist my calves around the pole – spinning with no hands.

Grabbing ahold again, I kick down to the ground and walk around the pole, needing to give Nico the best show of his fucking life. No matter who he's seen on this stage, or any other, he's going to remember me up here.

I keep my eyes on him with every move I make, and watch him as he clenches his jaw, fists his hands on his thighs, and spreads them again, trying to adjust himself.

A slow smile spreads across my face. I'm enjoying teasing him.

Nico's eyes fall to half-mast and he rubs his thumb over his bottom lip. Knowing he's turned on, it fuels me to go harder and sexier, and I lose myself in the moment.

When I'm down on my knees again, I crawl towards him, and at the end of the stage, I spread my knees apart and arch all the way back so my head is touching the floor.

I slowly drag myself back up, and when I snap my head forward, I'm met with the man who's haunted me nightly, standing right in front of me.

I freeze.

Our eyes are locked, and his are ablaze with desire.

I know he still wants me.

I can see it. I can feel it.

He cleared the club out the moment he saw me so no one else would see me dance. He wants me for his eyes only, and for the moment, I can give that to him.

I want him again as much as his eyes are telling me he wants me. I want to tease him until he breaks, though. I want to show him what he's been missing.

I want to feel like I did when I was with him before. Like a pretty princess who's being worshipped and debased at every available moment.

On my knees before him, we're almost eye-level, and I reach out, wanting to touch him. But I can't yet. Instead, I push myself away and slide towards the pole. I reach back and grab it, spinning around and up onto my feet again.

Nico remains standing at the end of the stage in a stance that can only be described as powerful and dominant. He's a man who gets his way and knows he's going to again now.

He crooks his pointer finger, beckoning me back to him, and once again, I obey without hesitation. Even when I'm up here, in control, he still has power over me.

I walk back to the edge of the stage and Nico grabs my wrist. He pauses for only a moment to caress my inner wrist with a back-and-forth swipe of his thumb before pulling me from the stage.

My breath leaves my lungs as I'm flung against his chest, and his other arm bands around my back while my legs instinctively wrap around his waist.

"You only dance for me now," Nico growls in my ear – his control waning.

Nico walks us backwards until we reach the chair he was sitting in and he sits us down. Every part of me is screaming to agree with him, but I can't. I'm dancing here for a reason.

"You don't get to tell me what to do," I counter, and he grips my chin, bringing my face to his.

Nico's eyes are hard as stone. His hands spread across my back and slide down to cup my ass, pushing me against his hard cock.

I let out a soft moan and he presses his fingers harder into my ass cheeks. "You only dance for me," he repeats, harsher this time.

"You're too late," I tell him, and he grunts, not liking my response.

Nico glides a finger up my spine, around my ribcage, between my breasts, across my collar bone, and back down my spine. I shiver in his arms and he grabs the ends of my hair, pulling my head to the side.

I gasp in surprise, and he trails his nose up the side of my exposed neck. He plants a kiss beneath my ear and I sigh. "I'm right on time, Cassandra," he says roughly.

Nico tugs on my hair again, this time pulling my head straight back, giving him the access he needs to run his nose down the front of my neck to plant a kiss in the hollow of my throat.

I bite my lip, holding in a soft moan, and Nico drags his nose up to my other ear. "Let me hear you purr like the pretty little kitten you are." He pulls the bow loose that's holding the front of my corset together. "You know I know how to make you purr." His hand on my ass squeezes me. "Let me hear you."

He kisses my ear again and bares his teeth, scraping them across my skin before biting down.

My moan is instant, turning into a mewling cry for more when he swirls his tongue around where he bit to ease the pressure.

"That's it, *la mia rossa piccante*," he whispers in my ear. "You're a good little kitty, aren't you?"

"Mmhmm," I hum, moving my hips against him.

Nico cups my pussy, pressing on the fabric that's separating us. "Now let me make this little kitty purr until my hand is covered in your sweet cream."

"Please," I say shamelessly, moving my hips to try and get him closer.

"You know I love when you beg, Cassandra."

Nico pulls my panties to the side and hooks his fingers through the holes in the fishnets I have on underneath.

He doesn't touch me yet, though.

He pulls his fingers away instead, but I can feel them trembling with the effort of not touching me.

I slide my hands down his chest and grip his shirt. "What are you waiting for, Nico?"

"That," he growls. "For you to say my name." He captures my lips with his in a searing kiss that has my mind wiped clear of everything but him.

Nico's long and thick middle finger slides right inside of me and I moan into our kiss, biting down on his lower lip, which has him groaning in return.

I love that sound. It's sexy and feral.

I bite harder to hear it again, and he adds a second finger inside me and presses his thumb against my clit in response.

I tear my lips from his and my head falls back to let out a throaty moan. He was the last man to touch me, and my hand and vibrator don't come close to this. To him.

Sliding my hands back up his chest to cup the sides of his neck, my inner muscles clench around his fingers, and I ride his hand.

"That's it, *la mia rossa piccante*. Ride my hand like the dirty little kitty I know you are. Use me."

I pry my eyes open and meet his dark ones. They make me feel alive, and it feels like he can see past every façade I'm wearing to the real me.

"More," I demand, and he adds a third finger – spreading them out inside me. I shudder and fall onto his hand, fully taking his fingers inside of me.

The moan that leaves me is a half scream, and Nico is quick to loosen the ribbon holding my corset together. Tearing it apart, his hot mouth latches onto my taut nipple.

I cry out, my nails instinctively digging into the nape of his neck as my pussy flutters around his fingers.

"Nico," I moan, and he sucks my other nipple into his hot, wet mouth. "Nico," I moan again, and he curls his fingers towards him inside me and swirls his thumb around my clit.

I'm almost...

"Let me see those eyes." I blink to clear the blurriness and focus on his brown eyes that are glowing like hot amber under the lights in here. "Come. Now."

Holding out until he says those magic words, my body listens like it's been trained by him. Like it only works for him now.

Damn him.

Fuck him.

I'm in pure fucking bliss and angry simultaneously, and I don't know why.

I press my forehead to his, and while I ride the waves flowing through me, Nico reaches up and unties the ribbon of my mask. That clears the fog pretty damn quickly, and I pull back, seeing the smug look of victory in his eyes.

My anger flares and I scramble off his lap. I do it too quickly, though, because my legs are still Jello from the earth-shattering orgasm he just gave me. I stumble back in my too-high heels until I crash into the stage.

Nico's smug look spreads into a grin that has my pussy contracting and throbbing for more. "Where are you going, Cassandra?" he asks. "You don't want me to see you? You want me to only see you like this? A stripper?" His gaze travels the length of my body. "Is that it?"

"Fuck you," I spit out, clutching my corset together with one hand.

Pushing off the stage, I walk as fast as I can to the dressing room, ripping off the stupid cat mask as I go. I'm not his pretty little kitty who does as he says.

Shit! Ow!

I forgot about the pins I had in my hair to keep it in place.

Oh well. The pain is helping to keep me level-headed and angry. Who does he think he is speaking to me like that? I don't care who he is. Him being a Carfano doesn't mean shit to me.

I know men like him. I grew up with them. And I'll be damned if I ever let one make me feel inferior.

I can feel him following me, but I ignore him. In the dressing room, I take off these stupid heels that are slowing me down and shove them in my bag before throwing on my sweats to cover myself.

I turn and see Nico leaning against the doorway. His face is devoid of emotion, but his eyes are speculative. I narrow mine and turn away from him to shove my hair products and makeup bag into my duffel. I slip my feet into my shoes and beeline for the back entrance I came through earlier tonight.

"Are you running from me?" he asks, amusement dancing in the notes of his voice.

"No," I say forcefully, gripping the strap of my bag tighter. Nico follows behind me, but it isn't until I'm outside that I remember I don't have a car anymore and need to order a rideshare.

"Shit," I mutter under my breath.

"Where's your car?"

Instead of answering him, I pull my phone out and open the app.

"Did you drive it here?"

"No," I clip, annoyed that he wants me to explain myself.

"I'll take you. Come on."

"No."

"Cassandra," he says, and I pause, finally looking up at him. "You're not taking a taxi from here alone. I'll take you home."

I look back down at my phone. "There's a car five minutes away. I'll wait."

Growling, Nico grabs my phone from my hand and my bag from my shoulder, and starts walking towards his car.

"What the hell are you doing?" I yell after him.

"Get in the car, Cassandra."

"I don't need your help, Nico."

That gets him to stop and turn back. "I'm taking you home. Get in the car."

CHAPTER 4
Nico

Once again, Cassandra fucking Connelly has me under a spell and acting like a damned animal when I don't mean to.

I wanted to rip her clothes off and fuck her against the stage after she gave me the best performance of my life just to show her what happens when she teases me like that. Then I wanted to drag her away and lock her in my apartment where no one will see her fiery side as she unravels every mystery clouded around her.

For me. *Only me.*

Cassie doesn't protest again after I told her to get in the car a second time. She just huffs out a lungful of air and walks to the passenger door where she eyes me suspiciously with her arms crossed.

Goddamn it, she's beautiful when she's mad.

I would love to have hate sex with her. I know she'd fucking come at me like a cat with her claws bared and ready for battle, and I'd gladly sacrifice myself and come out the other side with scratches knowing she gave me everything like she had something to prove.

Then, I'd want to have makeup sex in the kitchen after feeding her, where I'd eat her for dessert before carrying her back to bed to fuck her slowly. She'd give me that little gasp she does when she's trying to hold back and is surprised when she can't, as she grips the sheets and moans long and low.

"What are you waiting for?" Cassie asks impatiently.

Oh, right. Jesus, I was lost there for a moment.

"Nothing," I grumble, and she rolls her eyes.

I open the passenger door for her and she begrudgingly gets in, crossing her arms over her chest again like I wasn't just sucking on her perfect cherry nipples ten minutes ago.

I place her bag on the seat behind me, but keep her phone in my pocket so she can't run away when I get to her place.

"Put your address in," I instruct, bringing up the GPS on the dash screen.

Cassie hesitates, then quickly types it in and goes back to crossing her arms and turning away from me to look out the window.

The drive to her place is a quiet ten minutes, and when I pull into the driveway of her duplex, she shifts in her seat, her eyes scanning the front of the house.

"Where's your car?" I ask, needing to break the silence. "Is someone borrowing it?" There's no car in the driveway, and I remember her having one. I walked her down to it after our weekend.

"No," she clips, her anger still going strong.

"Are you mad at me?" I ask in a tone I know she'll respond to.

"Give me my phone."

"Not until you tell me why you're so mad and where your car is."

"Why are you so fixated on my car?"

"Why are you being so secretive about it?"

"I'm not. I just…" she pauses, trying to find a good lie I assume.

"You just…" I say, wanting her to finish her sentence.

"Stop that." Her eyes snap to mine, blazing blue like hot flames.

"Stop what?"

"That. Trying to get information from me I clearly don't want to share or want you to know. My life is none of your business."

"It's a simple question."

"With a complicated answer."

I soften my tone so she won't explode on me when I ask, "Did something happen to it? Do you need a new one?"

"What I need is my phone and my bag so I can get out of this car. This was a mistake. What happened back there was a mistake."

"Not for me," I tell her seriously, and her eyes narrow, trying to see if I'm for real or not. "I got what I wanted."

That was a mistake.

I meant I got what I wanted, which was more of her. But of course, it didn't come out that way.

Cassie's jaw clenches and her eyes grow angrier.

"I'm sure you did." She stretches into the back seat and grabs her bag. "Give me my phone."

I don't think I can fuck this up further, but I don't want to let her go like this with no prospect of seeing her again.

"Nico," she says forcefully, placing her hand palm-up in the air between us.

I take it in mine and turn it over. Cassie's eyes grow wide as I bring her hand to my mouth and kiss her knuckles. I can see her anger dissipate before my eyes. Her face and eyes soften to reveal her true feelings.

I knew it. I see it.

My eyes never leave hers as I turn her hand back over and kiss her palm. She melts further for me.

I place her phone in her hand and reluctantly let go.

Cassie can be mad all she wants, but I know her better than she thinks.

She swallows hard and whispers, "Thank you."

"I'll see you soon," I tell her, and before she can think about it, she replies automatically.

"Okay."

I can't help my smile as she climbs out of my car, knowing she probably wouldn't have agreed if I hadn't distracted her.

Cassie walks the short path from the driveway to the porch, and looks over her shoulder when she reaches the door on the left side of the duplex.

She digs through her bag for her keys, and her brows furrow as she comes up empty. I'm about to get out of the car to help, but she knocks on the door.

Does she live with someone?

Cassie quickly looks over her shoulder, checking to see if I'm still here, when the door opens and a man is standing there.

What the fuck?

The porch light illuminates his face, and it's clear someone just recently used him as a punching bag.

Cassie's hands fly to her mouth and she frantically looks over at me again before pushing the guy into the house and slamming the door closed.

Who the fuck is this guy?

Pulling out my phone, I dial Stefano. I need answers.

"Hey, Nico, what's up?"

"I need your help."

"Alright, one second. Let me get my laptop." I'm lucky he chose to stay the night at The Aces after the meeting, and lucky he doesn't go out or sleep much. "Okay, what do you need?"

"I need you to tell me who the guy at Cassandra Connelly's place is."

Stef is good in that he doesn't ask questions. I can hear him typing away, finding out what I need without needing to know the reason. Whatever any of us need, no matter how crazy our request, Stef gets it for us without judging our level of insanity.

"She inherited the duplex from her aunt that passed away last year. She does have a younger brother, Sean, whose last known address was in New York. It could be him."

I rub my eyes in relief while my jealousy wanes. He must be her brother.

"Are there any problems with him? He answered the door and clearly had the shit beaten out of him. Most likely tonight by the surprised look on Cassie's face when she saw him. I don't want whatever he's involved in to touch her."

"Yeah, give me a minute."

Stef goes quiet again as he does his thing, and I don't take my eyes off the house. I'm not leaving until I know she's safe.

"He's not in the system for anything. He's barely on the grid. No job, no apartment, no car. Nothing."

"Shit."

"My thoughts exactly. He used to have a little money to his name, but that dried up a few months ago. If he got the shit beaten out of him, then it's not for anything good."

"Or legal."

"Want me to dig deeper into them and see if I find anything?"

Yes.

"No," I sigh. "She's already pissed at me. I don't want to add fuel to the fire when she finds out I've been digging into her life without her knowing."

"Alright. Let me know if you change your mind."

"I will. Thanks, Stef."

"Sure."

We hang up, and I take a breath to calm down. If I wanted, I could have a packet of Cassie's entire life in my hands by the morning, but that's unfair to her.

I dial the manager of Dark Horse next, needing to fix one problem at a time. "Hello?"

"Sam, it's Nico."

"What can I do for you?"

"You can fire Cassandra. She no longer works at Dark Horse. I don't want you to ever let her in those doors again unless she's with me. Do you understand?"

"Yes, Sir."

"Good. And if she asks why, you can tell her it's because of me."

"Yes, Sir," he repeats.

"When did she start working there?" I ask, needing to know how many men have seen my girl looking as sexy as she did tonight. My blood fucking returns to boiling.

"Tonight was her first night, actually. She came in to audition earlier in the week. She said she hadn't worked at a club before, so I was skeptical, but then she surprised me."

"Just tell her she's fired," I order.

Sam clears his throat, knowing he crossed the line. "Yes, Mr. Carfano."

Hanging up, I close my eyes and rub the bridge of my nose. Thank fucking God tonight was her first night. I couldn't stand the thought of all those assholes watching her and getting to see what I saw. I think I'd go on a murder spree across the city.

I'm selfish that way, I guess. I want what I want, and I don't want anyone else to have it.

Next, I dial Alec. "Hey, Nico, what do you need?"

"I need you to put a car outside of someone's house."

"Why are you calling me for that?"

"Because she's in Atlantic City, not New York City."

"She? Who?"

"Cassandra Connelly."

"Okay, who is she? What's going on?"

"She's Lexi's friend. Something's going on with her brother and I need a car outside her house to make sure whatever he's into or whoever he fucked over doesn't come for him here. I want her safe."

"Why didn't you call Vinny if she's Lexi's friend?"

"Because I don't want him to give me shit about it, and I don't want him to tell Lexi."

"Fine. Text me her address and I'll send someone over."

"Good. I'll wait until he comes."

"Do you need me to look into what her brother's into?"

"No, I've got that covered."

"Alright."

Hanging up, I back out of Cassie's driveway and drive down the block, only to turn around and park across the street and a few houses down so she thinks I left.

It takes about fifteen to twenty minutes for a car to pull up behind me, and I get out to talk to him.

"You're watching that house there." I point to Cassie's. "If anyone comes or goes out of the door on the left, or if there's anything or anyone suspicious, call me. Don't be seen if you can help it, but intervene in anything if you need to. The woman is the priority, understand? She has red hair. You'll know it's her."

"I understand."

"Give me your number." He prattles off his number and I text him so he has mine. "And your name?" I ask as an afterthought.

"Rocco."

"I'm trusting you, Rocco. Don't let me down."

"I won't."

I nod my agreement and take one last look at her house before climbing in my car and driving back to The Aces.

After a hot shower, I lie down and stare at the ceiling. The minutes pass by until I can't take it anymore. I grab my phone and text Cassie.

Me: Night, Cassandra.

I want her to know I'm thinking of her and I want her to have my number. I had Stefano look it up and give it to me after our weekend together, but I haven't used it yet. That doesn't mean I haven't thought about it, though.

I want to make sure she's okay, I want her to tell me what's going on, and I want her to ask me for help.

Fuck.

I'm fucked.

Getting up, I go to the mini fridge and pull out three small bottles of whiskey and pour them all into a glass. I check my phone again. She's read it, but she hasn't responded.

Cassie is the only one who's successfully gotten me – the most level-headed of the family – to go just a little crazy. And after tonight, a lot crazy.

I collapse into one of the club chairs by the window and look down at the boardwalk lights flashing – memories of when I was a kid flickering on the periphery of my mind. When my dad ran The Aces, Vinny and I had Atlantic City as our playground when we came to visit. We would run around the boardwalk playing games, eating fried food, and going on rides until one of us threw up. Usually Vinny.

We had fun, Vinny and I. Dad always let us do whatever we wanted when we were here because he knew how strict our lives back in New York were. I used to hate that we lived apart, but I understood why. He wanted us to go to school with our cousins, and train and learn the family business alongside them.

We lived with our mom in an apartment in our family's building in the city. When Vinny graduated high school, he moved to AC to work with Alec and our dad to learn the business here. He loves it. I, on the other hand, prefer New York. That city made me the man I am, and being Leo's right-hand man, and third in command, is the job I know I'm best suited for.

I'm mostly by myself, I don't have the weight of the family on my shoulders 24/7, I don't run a small city, and I get to make sure my family is safely heading in the right direction.

It's not that Leo doesn't have a level head himself. Same with Luca, his brother and underboss. I'm just the quiet man two steps to the side and behind them that's there when they need me.

We all carry the power of the Carfano name.

No matter our position or role we play, each of us – every immediate descendant to my father and uncles and aunts – carries power.

But with power, comes a target on your back. And with that, comes an isolation within your family and a lack of trust for anyone else. A result of that, is a loneliness I've only known to fill with women who I get close enough to to fuck, but then it's over and I move on to the next. I never see a woman for longer than a night. I don't want them to get attached, and I certainly don't want to get attached.

But then Cassandra happened, and I haven't been the same since. I broke my rules and got attached. I spent the whole weekend with her and became addicted.

I check my phone every few minutes, waiting for her response, but nothing comes.

I send a quick text to the guy watching her, and he promptly replies that there's been no movement in or around her house thus far.

That's good, and I relax for a minute. But after another mini bottle of whiskey, I pick up my phone and stare at my message to her. I want her to know I'm not letting her go this time.

Me: I'm here if you need me.
Cassie: Why do you think I need you for something?

I smile down at my phone. She answered quickly this time.

Me: You tell me. I saw him when you opened the door. I just want to make sure you're safe.
Cassie: I am. Don't worry about me. I'm not your concern.
Me: But you are.
Cassie: I'm really not.
Me: Cassandra.
Cassie: Nico, why are you texting me right now? How did you even get my number? I never gave it to you.
Me: I have my ways.
Cassie: You could've just asked me.
Me: Would you have given it to me?
Cassie: No.
Me: Then I did the right thing.
Cassie: Why are you choosing to use it now?
Me: How do you know I haven't almost used it every day since I watched you drive off after that weekend?

She doesn't answer me right away this time. I stunned her with that one, I guess.

I wait three minutes, and she still doesn't reply.

Not this time, *piccante*.

I press the call button.

"Hello?" her soft voice filters through the phone after ringing three times, and my dick is instantly hard.

"Hi, Cassandra."

CHAPTER 5

Cassie

How do you know I haven't almost used it every day since that weekend?

Is he serious? How can he just drop that on me so casually?

My brain tries to come up with some kind of intelligent response, but I've got nothing. I'm blank.

A few minutes pass, and I'm still stuck staring at my phone when it starts to buzz.

He's calling me.

My heart starts racing at the thought of hearing his voice right now.

A part of me doesn't want to answer because of that, but the other, larger part of me, wants to hear his voice right now.

It's probably not a good idea, and I shouldn't indulge myself in what I know is a bad idea, but tonight hasn't exactly been going the way I thought it would, so screw it.

I swipe my finger across my screen to answer. "Hello?"

"Hi, Cassandra." Nico's voice floats over the line and I feel it pool in my stomach like liquid gold – a divine burn. "I wasn't sure you'd answer."

"Why wouldn't I?" I'm not about to admit that I wasn't sure I would or should. "Maybe I wanted you to hear my voice when I told you to stop texting me."

"Maybe. But I'll bet any amount you'd like that you're lying in bed right now and contemplated answering because you were afraid that hearing my voice would be too much for you."

My jaw drops. The audacity of this man. "Wow, you're really full of yourself. What makes you believe your voice is so special it would be hard to hear while I'm lying in bed?"

"So, you are lying in bed right now?"

"Are you serious?"

"Yes," he assures me, the low timbre of his voice making me bite my lip. I knew this was a mistake. "So, are you?" he asks seductively, and I curl onto my side, holding my phone tighter to my ear.

"Yes," I whisper, and Nico makes a little grunt of a sound like he pulled the phone away so I wouldn't hear him. "Is that a problem?"

"Yes, because now all I can think about is your flawless skin in the dim glow of the moon as I trace the curves of your body until your dripping wet and begging me to take care of you. First with my mouth so I can taste your moon drenched skin and honey on my tongue, and then I'd bury my cock in your magic pussy that will take me to the fucking stars and back. I want to hear your muffled scream of my name into the pillows as I fuck you from behind, and then feel you rake your nails down my back when your next scream is stuck in your throat and your blue eyes are staring into mine. I could drown in your eyes and I'd die a happy man."

Holy fuck.

Is he real?

"I could keep going, Cassandra, but then I'll be stuck with an even bigger problem than I have going on right now, and I only have my hand to take care of it and not your hot little mouth or tight little pussy."

Oh, my God, he has to stop.

I pinch my eyes closed and rub my thighs together, trying to focus on not drowning in my own desire.

"Nico," I whisper, knowing my voice can't be trusted.

"Yeah, *piccante?*"

"You can't…you can't say things like that."

"Why not?"

"Are you drunk?"

"No. Do you think I need to be drunk in order to tell you how much I want you?"

"I thought we said just that one weekend. Nothing more."

"We did. But I don't agree to that anymore."

"You don't?"

"No."

I swallow the lump in my throat and push every feeling of hope down. I can't let it bubble up. I can't let myself believe that Nico wants me.

I know what men like him are capable of. What they've done and will do. I also know how quickly they can turn on you and cut you off like you never meant a thing when you were once considered family.

I don't trust men like him.

Then again, I don't have to trust him with anything other than my body in order to receive the greatest orgasms of my life. My heart can fully remain safely behind the wall I built a long time ago.

"I'm not going to date you, Nico," I tell him, hoping he'll understand.

He pauses, then says, "I never said anything about dating, *piccante*. I just want more of you. Can you give me that?"

"Maybe."

"Tomorrow. I can pick you up or you can come to me."

"Who said I was free tomorrow?" I challenge, not wanting him to think I'm clearing my schedule for him.

"You can't give me a few hours? I promise to make it worth it," he says low, the thrum of his voice hitting me in my already throbbing core.

"Maybe a few. But only in the afternoon."

"An afternoon delight." He chuckles deeply. "Good. The sooner the better."

I love hearing how much he wants me. It's sexy, and the best reason to agree to see him again.

"I'll meet you there."

"I'm in the same room as last time. I'll let the front desk know and they'll let you up. But can you do something for me, Cassandra?" Anything, as long as he keeps saying my name like that.

"Mmhmm."

"When you hang up with me and slide your hand inside your panties to touch that pretty wet pussy of yours, know I'll be gripping my cock, picturing you spread open on my bed, begging me to fill you with my cock and to fuck you until you can't remember your name."

A choked moan leaves my throat and I rub my thighs together, needing to do exactly that. But he's not going to end this call thinking he has the upper hand.

"Who said I'm wearing panties? Who said I'm wearing anything at all?" I ask, keeping my voice soft and breathy to drive him crazy. "In fact," I pause, sliding my hand under the blanket, "I had just finished showering and applying lotion before crawling into bed when you called. My skin is soft and smooth, and I was just about to…" I trail off intentionally, reaching into my bedside table's drawer.

"Just about to what?" he asks, his voice strained and eager.

"Use my little friend that never lets me down." I turn on my vibrator and hold it to my phone so he can hear the soft buzz. "Goodnight, Nico. I'll see you tomorrow at noon."

"Cassandra–" I hang up before he can say anything else. I only needed to hear my name in that deep growl of his one last time to get me started. My vibrator can take care of the rest. For tonight, at least.

I wake sometime later after the best orgasm I've had without a man – Nico – giving it to me, to see a text from him.

Nico: You'll pay for that.

Nico: And bring that little friend of yours tomorrow.

I drift off again with a smile on my lips. I can't wait for my punishment.

CHAPTER 6

Cassie

I didn't set an alarm, so I wake up later than I wanted, but I needed the sleep. Especially with the long day ahead of me.

Rolling out of bed, I put on the sweatpants and t-shirt I had thrown over the back of the chair in the corner of my room, and make my way downstairs to the kitchen. My throat is so dry, I down two glasses of water before I even start a pot of coffee and cook breakfast.

I make pancakes, eggs, and bacon – my brother's favorites. Sean scared me last night when he opened the door and I saw him covered in cuts and bruises. He wouldn't let me look at any of his wounds and refused to go to the hospital to be looked at. I'm pretty sure he has a few broken ribs.

I love my brother. He's all I have left. But I also hate him for what he's gotten himself into.

Sean's four years younger than me and doesn't remember our life in Boston the way I do.

Our dad was a member of the McLaughlin family. When I was twelve, he sat me down and told me that if he didn't help the feds in a case against the family, then he'd go to prison. If he helped, then my brother, me, and him, would go into witness protection.

He lasted all of five days under federal protection before the family found him and killed him, along with the three agents he was with when they were on their way to the FBI offices in Boston.

Agents promised twelve-year-old me that they would protect my dad. Well, it ended just as quickly as it began, and my brother and I were sent to Atlantic City to live with our Aunt Sloane, our dad's sister.

Sean was still only eight, so I tried to keep an eye on him as best as I could so we wouldn't be too much of a burden to our aunt. She went from being single and free, to having two kids move in with her that she barely saw before that point.

She had nothing to say about our father's death, but for ten years, the three of us were a little family who stuck together. Sean and I started our lives over and tried our best to make the most of it.

It worked for those ten years, until our aunt died last year in a car accident, and Sean went quiet. He acted like nothing happened, but I knew he had to be hurting. He was denied a mother figure twice in his life.

So, when he told me he was going to move to the city for college, I was stupid enough to think he wanted a fresh start of his own. But while I was made to believe he was going to school, he was really befriending the New York faction of the McLaughin family and gambling away all the money our dad left us that he got access to when he turned eighteen.

He showed up two weeks ago, asking for money and a place to lay low while he figured things out. It turns out he gave up on school within the first few weeks and decided drinking and gambling was a better fit for him. He said he thought he finally found a place to belong. A place where his name was known and he felt connected to his lost childhood. But it was a lie.

He didn't say anything more.

I sold my car for quick cash and gave the money to Sean to give to them.

After our dad was killed, Aunt Sloan sold everything in Boston and divided the money between Sean and I so we'd have something when we were older. But between college tuition, the car I bought, car insurance, and just general life needs, I don't have much left to offer Sean. It helped me not have to work while I went to school, too.

Aunt Sloan owned this duplex and she left it to me in her will, but I use the rent the neighbors pay for property tax and repairs, so I really don't have anything from that to give Sean and the assholes who let him run up a massive debt. He gambled his portion away just a handful of months into being on his own. Tens of thousands of dollars gone with nothing to show for it aside from bruises and death threats. Which is why I took the job at the club. I need cash, and I need it fast.

I head back upstairs and knock on Sean's door tentatively.

"What?" he asks, annoyed.

"I made breakfast if you want some. Your favorites."

"Can you bring it to me?"

"No. I want to talk about what happened."

"I don't want to talk, Cass. There's nothing to talk about. They found me last night and let me know very loudly that I can't run from them."

Sighing, I rest my forehead against the door. "How much time do we have?"

Sean doesn't answer right away, and I'm about to ask again when he finally says, "A week. And now they want an extra twenty grand for the trouble of having to find me."

An extra twenty?

He already gave five thousand after I sold my car, and I was being optimistic when I thought we could pay in installments. I was also being optimistic when I thought dancing would bring in a couple thousand a week if I worked almost every day. But a week to pay a hundred grand? That's not enough time.

"We'll figure it out, Sean."

"Cassie, there's nothing to figure out. I'm a dead man in a week. We don't have that kind of money."

"Don't say that," I say quickly. "I can try and sell the house. I can do something. Don't give up."

"You can't sell this place fast enough."

"Don't give up," I repeat, and the door flies open, making me stumble away.

"I am, Cass," he hisses, and I gasp at the sight of him. He looks terrible. His entire face is swollen and bruised, with cuts over his eyebrows, lip, and cheeks, and bruises all over his torso.

"Then you have to run. Go as far as you can so they can't find you."

"They found me here, which means they'll find you here even when I'm not. I'm not letting them touch you, Cass. This is my mess, not yours."

Tears well in my eyes. "We'll face it together. I'm going to do what I can to help you. No matter what, okay? You're my brother, Sean. It's just me and you now, and I'm not going to lose you."

Sean looks defeated, but he pulls me in for a hug, and I gently wrap my arms around him so I don't hurt him.

"I love you, Cass. I'm sorry."

"I love you, too."

I know he's sorry. I know he wishes we were dealt a different hand in life, but so do millions of other people. I've tried to make the most of what I have, and remind myself to keep pushing through no matter what. This is just another bump in the road. I'm not giving up on the only family I have left.

CHAPTER 7
Nico

Cassie knocks on my door a little after noon, and goddamn, she's beautiful. Her red hair is wavy today and cascades down from her head like a wall of silk. I reach for it without thinking, rubbing it between my fingers to feel how soft it is.

I look into her bright blue eyes and notice they're extra guarded today, with a hint of sadness. I open my mouth to ask her what's wrong, but she grabs the front of my shirt and pulls me towards her as she lifts up on her toes to meet me halfway – silencing whatever I was about to say with a kiss.

Whatever she has on her mind, she clearly wants to forget, and I can definitely help her with that. My one hand dives into her hair while my other takes her waist, dragging her inside my room.

With the click of the door closing, I lift Cassie up, and she wraps her legs around my hips. It's déjà vu as I walk her back to my bedroom, except this time, I know exactly what I'm in for.

Cassie kisses me like I'm her source of air and she's drowning, desperate for more. She claws at the back of my neck and runs her fingers up my scalp.

Fuck, that feels good.

I groan into her mouth and she tightens her legs around me.

In my room, I waste no time, and throw us both down on top of my bed, deepening our kiss until Cassie is writhing beneath me, trying to find any friction she can.

I make quick work of ridding her of her sweater, jeans, and shoes, and take a moment to look down at her and commit to memory her flushed skin, swollen lips, and pulse jumping out of her neck.

She's effortlessly sexy.

It's engrained in everything she does.

But her in a matching light pink bra and panties? *Fuck me.* She knows how to drive me crazy.

"This color looks good on you, *piccante*." Her eyes lighten and then narrow, and I grin. "Not in the mood for compliments, I see." She shakes her head. "Or talking." She shakes her head again.

"We both know why I'm here."

"Maybe I want to hear it," I challenge, scraping my teeth over my bottom lip – a movement her eyes follow with heated attention.

Her blue eyes pierce mine. "Fuck me, Nico."

"No sweeter words have ever been spoken." I wink, and make quick work of my clothes, tossing them on the floor with hers. Standing above her, I grip my cock in my hand and she licks her lips, her eyes once again following my every move.

Being the impatient little minx that she is, Cassie reaches behind her back and unclasps her bra, pulling it from her body and tossing it to the side.

"That's my job, *piccante*."

"You weren't fast enough. You were staring again."

I try and hide my smile by gliding my hand across my lips and chin, but she sees it and cups her perfect tits in her hands – squeezing and pushing them together.

"If you're going to keep laughing at me, I'll start without you and you can watch all you'd like without touching me the way I know you want to."

Goddamn it.

The smile is wiped from my face and I grab her ankles, dragging her down the bed. She gasps, and I wrap my hands around her wrists, pinning them to her sides.

"You're testing my control," I tell her, hovering above her.

Cassie arches her back, pressing her soft tits against my chest. "That was the point." I tighten my grip on her wrists. "I want you in control. But if you're not up for it, I can always use my little friend I brought and you can sit over there and watch."

"Where is it?"

"In my purse that fell somewhere."

I release her and pick her bag up. I know better than to go inside a woman's purse, but Cassie doesn't want a gentleman right now.

It takes me all of two seconds to find her pink vibrator and I hold it up, looking back at her to see a look of confusion flicker through her eyes. Has no one ever used a toy on her, *for her*?

Oh, babygirl, I'm going to show you how in control of you I am.

"Suck," I command, holding the vibrator up to her lips. She opens without question and takes it in her mouth. I glide a single finger down the center of her chest and stomach.

Cassie hums and moves her hips, lifting them when I pull her pink panties down her long, toned legs. She spreads her legs apart and I push her vibrator deep into her mouth and back out.

Her pussy is glistening, but I want it fucking dripping for me. I pull the vibrator from her mouth and turn it on, the low hum of the first setting making my cock jump as I'm dragging it down her body – circling her tits, hard nipples, belly button, and glide it through her wet folds.

"Ohhh," she moans, lifting her hips, trying to get more. I press my hand to her lower stomach and push her back down to the bed.

"You get what I give you, Cassandra." Her eyes flare and she bites her lip. "Got it?"

"Yes," she sighs, and I reward her with another pass of the silicone through her pussy, this time pressing down on her clit. She shudders and moans, gripping the sheets beside her.

I climb up onto the bed with her and spread her legs wider so I can circle her entrance with the tip of the vibrator – teasing her until her pussy drips for me.

"Nico." She moans my name so fucking beautifully that I reward her again. I circle her clit, over and over, increasing the vibration setting each time until her moans turn to little gasps and then screams, which is when I plunge her vibrator at its highest setting inside her pussy.

Cassie's eyes fly open and find mine. Hers are filled with everything I need and remember. She walked in here with a purpose and her guard up, but it's down now, and I love seeing her free. I love knowing I made her so fucking crazy, she couldn't keep ahold of her control anymore. Which, I suspect, is why she came to me.

"Is this how you felt last night after you hung up on me?" I tease, twisting the vibrator to make her gasp.

She shakes her head frantically. "No. You've ruined this for me too," she says angrily, and I flash her a triumphant grin.

"What else have I ruined for you?"

Cassie's cheeks stain pink with a mixture of anger and embarrassment that she slipped up and admitted that. And just when I thought she couldn't get any more beautiful…

I should tell her she ruined me too, but I'm loving this moment too much to let her turn the tables on me.

"You don't want to answer, *la mia rossa piccante*, and that's fine. I already know. And guess what?" I ask, looking deep into her eyes as I press on her clit. "I'm going to ruin you further."

I can tell she's about to say some smartass remark, so before she has the chance, I pull the vibrator from her and flip her onto her stomach. I pull her hips up and back so I have a view of both her pretty pink pussy and tight puckered asshole that I can't wait to fuck. But not today. Today, I'm going to show her how good it can be if I did.

Her style of vibrator is perfect for what I want to do.

I plunge it back inside her to drench it in her juices even more before dragging it up to her tight little hole.

I lower the vibration intensity and Cassie tenses, making a little garbled grunt into the comforter.

"Relax, Cassandra," I murmur, leaning down to kiss her perfectly round ass. "Let me make you feel good. I promise you'll come so hard you'll forget you're mad at me for ruining you. In fact, you'll be thanking me."

"Fuck you," she grumbles, and I smile.

"No, *la mia rossa piccante*, I'm going to fuck *you*. Hard. The way you need it." I rub her ass cheek and then slap it, using the opportunity to push at the vibrator while she's momentarily distracted.

"Ohmygod," she strings together in a rush, her fists gripping the comforter like she's bracing for the worst.

I pause, letting her adjust to the new feeling. I reach between her and rub her clit, needing her to relax, and she does immediately. I keep circling her clit until she's mewling like the good little kitty she is and I feel her muscles relax enough for me to slide the vibrator in halfway.

Cassie cries out and I plug her pussy with my thumb while pressing down on her clit with my middle finger. Her pussy flutters around my thumb, trying to get more of me, so I push the vibrator in the rest of the way. She moans, pushing her ass back at me to take it all like a good girl.

Leaning over her, I move her hair over her shoulder and whisper in her ear, "Stay just like this. Don't move an inch. If you do, you won't get my cock in your pussy with the vibrator in your ass. Which would be a shame since I know how much you'll love the feeling of being so full. Wouldn't you like that? To be full?"

Once again, she answers me with a garbled moan and a nod.

I lick her ear and bite down on her lobe. "Good girl," I whisper. "Stay just like this."

Leaving her, I grab a condom from my nightstand and take a look at how gorgeous she is in this position for me. Better than my dreams. Better than every fantasy. Better than my memory. She's better than all of it.

I roll the condom down my length and position myself behind her again, nudging at her entrance.

She moans and presses back against me again.

So eager.

I up the vibrator by one level and push inside her slowly, wanting her to feel every inch of me filling and stretching her to capacity.

So fucking good.

A relief to finally be where I've wanted to be for so long washes over me, but it's quickly replaced with the insane need to chase the bliss I know she can give me.

Cassie is clawing at the comforter, and her unintelligible sounds of pleasure make me feel like a fucking king. To drive a woman with a smartass mouth and attitude like hers to a garbled mess of moans, half spoken words, cries, and pleas to deities is the ultimate ego boost.

I thrust in the rest of the way and look down at where we're connected. So fucking sexy. Especially with the end of her vibrator sticking out of her ass, too.

Gathering her hair, I wrap it around my fist and pull her head to the side.

"I want to hear you scream, Cassandra. I want the whole floor to know exactly what we're doing and how much you love having both your holes filled at the same time." She lets out a choked squeal and I pull her hair again. "Is that a yes?"

"Yes!" she exclaims, squeezing her pussy around my cock. "As long as you give me a reason to scream."

"You know I will. But now I'm thinking I should've stuffed my cock down your throat first to tame that tongue of yours." I lean down and whisper in her ear, "Next time."

Cassie grunts. "Just fuck me. I already know you like when I can't talk with your cock in my mouth, but I don't remember if you like my pussy. You should remind me."

Her claws are out, and I fucking love it. I can't resist a challenge, and I love when she talks dirty.

"Oh, you know I like your pussy." I pull out just a few inches and thrust back in quickly, making her gasp. "But I have no problem reminding you just how much."

Releasing her hair, I grip her hip and keep my other on the end of the vibrator, needing to drive her to her limit before she gives in to me.

I pull out almost all the way and slam back inside, loving the little scream she gives me. "You'll never forget again, *piccante*."

I know I'm not going to last long. Not when I've been dreaming of this for over a month. Over a month of my hand. Over a month of nothing but my desperation for her and a repeat of this.

Cassie does that squeezing thing with her pussy again and it unleashes me. I don't hold back. I can't.

Fucking Cassie is as close to heaven as I know I'll ever get with all the shit I've done, and I refuse to take it for granted or let the chance for this to be my every day slip through my fingers a second time.

I start to fuck her ass with her vibrator in tandem with me, and I'm rewarded with her pussy flooding my cock.

"That's it, Cassandra," I praise, and she squeezes around me. I know she loves when I say her full name. "You're taking me so well. My cock looks so good coated in your come."

She moans and fucks me back harder. She braces herself on her elbows so she can rock back faster, and I can fuck her back even harder.

I press the button on her vibrator to turn it up to the max setting and Cassie goes fucking feral. Her moans grow louder and she cries out with each thrust into her.

I want to come with her, and I know she's close. I can feel her pussy pulsing around me while the fire starts to burn its way down my spine.

Damn it, I wish I didn't have a condom on. I want to feel her pussy bare. I want my come to fill her and have her leaking my seed for hours afterwards.

"Nico…" she moans, and I groan, feeling the vibrations of my name run through her and straight into me.

"Say it again," I demand. "Tell everyone who's fucking you," I growl out.

Crying out, she gasps, then moans, "Nico."

"Not loud enough, *piccante*."

"Nico!" she shouts, but it's still not what I need.

I thrust into her one, two, three more times, and slide my hand around from her hip to her pussy and find her swollen, hard clit, and rub tight circles around it.

Cassie shakes as a moan gets stuck in her throat, and I know I have her.

I twist the vibrator inside her and slam into her one last time while simultaneously pulling the vibrator from her ass and pressing down on her clit.

I let out a guttural groan that comes from the pits of hell while she screams my name from the same place, "NICO!"

Exactly what I fucking wanted.

Her pussy is squeezing me like a vise and making me see fucking stars as I come so hard, it feels like I'll shoot right through the condom.

I fall to the bed beside her and pull her on top of me, needing to keep her as close as possible before she has the chance to push me away. I feel her racing heart beating rapidly against my chest like a hummingbird's wings, and it makes mine flutter the same in response.

Unless it's hers matching mine?

CHAPTER 8
Cassie

The fog lifts and my eyes open. I have to blink a few times though before everything's clear, and I'm met with Nico's broad chest. My cheek rests above his heart, and the steady, strong beat calms my own from getting out of control.

My arm is draped over him, so I carefully lift it up and scoot away.

"No," he grumbles in his sleep, and I smile.

"I'll be right back," I whisper, kissing his chest, and his arm around me relaxes so I can get up.

Standing next to the bed, I take a moment to admire him in all his glory. Goddamn, he's beautiful. He's built strong and solid. Like if he took on the world, he'd win.

I pick up the button-down shirt he was wearing last night from the floor and shrug it on. His scent envelopes me, and I bring the collar to my nose for a deep inhale, hoping I never forget it.

I spot my vibrator on the floor and my cheeks heat. I pick it up, along with my purse, and tip-toe to the bathroom. Leaning against the closed door, I take another deep breath.

What he did…

What we did…

I…

I'm literally at a loss for words, which is something that rarely happens. I usually have too many words. But Nico has rendered me speechless, and I know the words 'holy shit' and 'amazing' don't even begin to cover it. Not even a little bit.

Shaking my head, I take a look in the mirror and my eyes widen.

"Oh my God," I breathe, then cover my mouth when a little laugh escapes. I look like I've been thoroughly fucked.

I place my things on the counter and wash my vibrator first, then shove it back in my purse before quickly using the toilet and fixing my hair and smudged makeup.

I'm sore everywhere. I know I'll be feeling it all night when I'm dancing, but maybe it'll give me the mindset I need to slip into when I'm up on stage. I'll imagine myself dancing for Nico again, and him fucking me like an animal against the stage.

That reminds me, I need to text Sam to apologize for last night and ask him for as many shifts as possible this week.

Me: Hey, Sam, it's Cassie. I'm sorry about last night. We can talk about it tonight when I come in if you want, but I promise it won't happen again.

Sam: Hi, Cassie. It's okay about last night. I understand. But you don't need to come in tonight.

Me: Oh, I thought this weekend was my trial period and you wanted me Friday, Saturday, and Sunday?

Sam: Yeah, I did say that. But last night was your first and last night. I'm sorry.

Me: Please, I need the money. I promise it won't happen again.

Sam: Look, Cassie, it's not my decision. Nico said you're fired, so you're fired. I'm sorry.

That motherfucker.

He had me fired?!

Who does he think he is?!

I throw the bathroom door open and startle Nico awake when it slams and bounces off the wall.

"What's wrong? Did something happen?" he asks frantically, looking around the room.

"Yes, something's wrong," I grind out. "You had me fired!"

"Oh, that." Nico's shoulders relax and he rubs his eyes, then runs his hands through his hair.

"Yes, *that*, you asshole! Who do you think you are getting me fired? You're the one who sent everyone away because your ego can't handle anyone else seeing me dance."

His face shutters closed and he climbs out of bed, approaching me with slow, deliberate steps, until my back is pressed against the wall.

"Who am I to have you fired?" He tilts his head and narrows his gaze. "I own that club. I can do whatever the fuck I want." Nico pinches my chin to make sure I see his eyes when he says, "And you're damn right I don't want anyone else seeing you dance. The world gets to see how fucking sexy and beautiful you are just by stepping outside each and every day, and I already can't stand that. So, yeah, I don't want anyone seeing you when you're showing them every man and woman's fantasy playing out right in front of them. You'd be responsible for a mass fucking murder, Cassandra. Do you want that? My hands covered in blood because I couldn't stand anyone looking at you the way I do?"

"You don't get to make that decision for me," I manage to say through my tight throat.

His close proximity is making my anger wane, and when what he said sinks in, I sag against the wall.

I can't back down, though.

I can't be that weak.

I steel my spine and press my hand against his chest so he keeps his distance. "I need that job. You're going to call Sam and tell him you made a mistake."

"I'm not doing that. I didn't make a mistake. I don't make mistakes."

"You're so arrogant!"

"For good reason," he says, his cockiness driving me crazy.

"Nico, I need the money. I need to work there."

"Why do you need money so badly?"

"That's none of your business."

"It is," he insists.

"How?" I challenge, and his jaw ticks.

"My club, my business."

I clench my jaw, keeping my mouth shut before I lose my shit. I take a deep breath in through my nose.

"Does it have anything to do with you no longer having a car?"

"Jesus fucking Christ!" I exclaim. "What is with you and my car? I sold my car last week, okay? Are you happy now that you know?"

"Yes, very," he says smugly. "Why did you sell it? Does it have to do with your brother and the fact that he's back in town and got the shit beaten out of him?"

"I don't owe you an–" I cut myself off. "Wait." I push on his chest to get him away from me, but he doesn't budge. "How do you know about my brother? Did you look into my life? My background? My family?"

"I drove you home and a half-beaten man answered the door. Yes, I looked into your life. I knew you weren't going to tell me."

"Nico, that's completely inappropriate. You can't do that," I tell him, nervous he might have found out too much.

"I can and I did. And I'll go deeper unless you tell me what's going on."

"My brother's in trouble and I'm helping him. That's all you need to know."

Nico's eyes search mine. "I can help."

"I don't want your help. I can figure things out on my own."

"Doesn't mean you have to. You don't have to do everything yourself."

"You don't know me like you think you do. I've been doing things on my own for a while now. Why stop now?"

"Since your aunt died last year, or before that?"

My heart sinks as the anger is wiped from me. "Are you kidding me?"

"I'm sorry. I'm sure she meant a lot to you. She took care of you when your dad died, right? What happened to your mother?"

"Why don't you tell me? You seem to know everything."

"Hardly. I want you to tell me."

"Yeah, well, I'd like to not be fired, have my car back, get my brother out of trouble, and not have come here today to only have to explain any of this to you. I just wanted to forget for a few hours, but you've ruined that." I push against him again, and he lets me move him away this time.

Finally, some air that's not filled with the faint remnants of his cologne or the close proximity of his naked body that's making me dizzy with need and filling my head with visions of everything we can do together.

"Put some damn clothes on," I tell him.

"You're wearing my shirt. How about you give it back?" He smirks, thinking he's clever.

I grab my clothes off the floor and close and lock myself in the bathroom. I quickly redress, and when I emerge again, he's still there, naked, and leaning against the wall beside the door with that dumb and sexy smirk still in place.

"Here." I press his balled-up shirt against his chest and his hand covers mine – caging me in his warm embrace.

"Don't go."

"I have to. I shouldn't have come here. It was stupid to think I could use you as a distraction."

"It's not stupid. I'll happily be your distraction. In fact, if you take your clothes off right now, I'll distract you for the rest of the day."

"That was the last time, Nico. I can't do this with you. Just leave me alone."

I walk towards the door of his hotel suite, but as I reach for the handle, Nico covers my hand with his again. "I can't leave you alone, Cassandra. I'll go mad."

"Then go mad." I shake his hand off and fling the door open.

My heart is racing. It's trying to go back to Nico as I lead it away from him.

I order a rideshare in the elevator so it's outside waiting for me by the time I get down there.

I need to remain calm. I need to think.

I'll have to find another job. I'll have to find another club to dance in if I'm going to make enough money to help Sean. Even if we can't get the full amount, getting close has to be good enough for now, right? Hopefully I can buy us another few weeks if I can show them I can eventually pay the full amount.

CHAPTER 9
Cassie

I tried to get my job back at Dark Horse yesterday despite Nico getting me fired, but I wasn't even let inside. The two bouncers at the door stopped me and I waited for Sam to come out to tell me he couldn't let me in under any circumstances. He did, however, pull me aside and reluctantly tell me that I should check out Pandemonium Gentleman's Club for a job. He gave me their number and told me he'd call the manager there and put in a good word.

I miss lazy Sunday mornings, where the only decision I needed to make that day was where I was ordering dinner from and what show or movies I was going to binge.

Now, I'm waking up just as stressed as I was when I went to sleep, with my stomach in knots, scared I won't have my brother here next weekend.

A hot shower loosens my sore muscles, and I lean against the tiled wall when I think of *him* and yesterday. I've never felt closer, yet still so far away from a person than I did yesterday.

He was just supposed to be some fun.

Before the night I met him, I was attempting the whole dating app thing. I was ready to try and find someone I could connect with and stave off the loneliness I was feeling, but it was a complete disaster. I went on an endless amount of first dates, and none of them ever amounted to anything past that.

Then I met Nico, and he's been the only man I've wanted to spend more time with, and actually *get to know on a deeper level,* in quite a long time. But at the same time, I know I shouldn't. I shouldn't get close to him. I shouldn't let him have influence over any aspect of my life – now or in the future.

I left that life behind when I was twelve, and it's only brought my brother trouble since he tried to get back into it.

My best friend, Lexi, is with Nico's brother, Vinny, and they're so in love it's disgusting. She tried to avoid him and tried not to like him, but Vinny has a charm about him that's hard to resist. They're good together. They understand one another. They complete and challenge each other in a way Lexi didn't know possible.

It's funny, considering she was the one who called me to warn me that Nico was a Carfano and I should be careful with him, when she's the one who fell head over heels for the guy she was trying to avoid.

"Hey, Cass?" Sean calls from downstairs.

"Yeah?"

"Do you have someone with you up there?"

"What? No, why?"

"Because there's a car in the driveway that I don't recognize. And I sure as hell know our neighbors aren't able to afford one like that."

I walk downstairs and find Sean in the living room, peering out the front window. "A car like what?" I ask.

"A brand new red Range Rover."

I stand next to him and look out at the driveway we share with our neighbors. They're a normal, middle-class family, with both parents being teachers at the local elementary school, and a son in middle school that keeps them busy with all the sports he's in. I doubt they could afford it either, but you never know where money comes from.

"Maybe they have a guest over. Why are you being so nosey?"

"I can't leave the house looking like this, so I need to get my fix of the outside world somehow."

Sean's bruises have gotten nastier and more prominent, and I know he must be in a world of pain.

"How about I let you pick where we order dinner from tonight?"

"Wow, you must really feel bad for me if you're going to give me free reign over food."

"Maybe," I concede, and drop the curtain back into place to go make coffee.

"Then I want Chinese."

I smile. "Perfect. Exactly what I was craving."

I sit down with my cup of coffee on the couch and watch the local news for a few minutes before putting on a station that's having a Fast and Furious marathon. I won't deny I have a weakness for Paul Walker and men who love fast cars.

It's a little while later that my phone vibrates with a text from Nico, and I'm not proud to say that my heart does a little stutter beat in my chest from excitement.

Nico: Did you look outside yet?"

Me: Yes…?

Nico: The color reminds me of you, so I knew you had to have it. The keys are in your mailbox.

Me: If you're saying you bought that car for me, then you're crazy.

Nico: Then I'm crazy.

Me: I'm not keeping it.

Nico: Yes, you are. It's yours. You said you wanted your car back.

Me: That didn't mean you needed to go out and buy me one. One that's worth at least ten times what mine was.

Nico: It's yours, Cassie. Drive it or don't, but it's yours.

He's crazy. He's fucking crazy.

I don't even know how he arranged something so quickly, but it's too much.

I can't keep it.

Can I?

No, I shouldn't. I can't be driving a hundred-thousand-dollar car when that's what I need to save Sean.

Oh, there's an idea…

But I still can't keep it, and I need Nico to know that this isn't okay.

Me: Nico, I can't be bought.

Nico: I'm not trying to buy you, Cassandra. It's in your name, so it's your choice what you do with it. Keep it, sell it, leave it sitting in your driveway until you decide it's just a car and you want to drive it. It's your choice.

That motherfucker.

He bought it for me knowing I had money problems.

Goddamn it.

He thinks he can be sneaky by helping me indirectly.

I have my pride that's telling me to drive it to The Aces and leave it parked there for him, but I know if I do that, he'll probably just drive it back to my house, and back and forth we'll go until one of us tires.

If he wants to spend an exorbitant amount of money for no reason, then who am I to stop him? Besides, it's for my brother. If Sean wasn't in trouble, then I would have a little fun playing with Nico. I just don't have time for games right now.

I can't tell Sean that it's my car or that I'm selling it for him. He's going to have way too many questions I don't want to answer. He already had a lot to say about me starting to dance to make money, but I told him it's the only chance we have to keep him alive and safe. He dropped the argument pretty quickly after that.

I wait for Sean to go upstairs again before going out to the mailbox to grab the keys and hide them in my purse. I won't deny it's a beautiful car, but it'll give us a big chunk of what we need, if not all of it, if I can sell it.

Sinking back into the couch, I close my eyes. My body and mind are tired. *So tired.*

CHAPTER 10

Cassie

I wake up early and quietly sneak out so Sean won't see me leave in the Range Rover.

This car is nice.

In fact, I love it.

It's too bad I can't keep it, because she drives like a dream and I could totally see myself in the summer with the windows down, wind blowing through my hair, and music up loud as I drive to a destination yet known.

But that's not my reality. I can't even see past the next few days, let alone think about a summer filled with good times and sunshine.

Late last night, I found a place that will buy my car for cash as early as today, but I'm going to the closest dealer that sells Range Rovers to see how much they'll offer me before I commit.

I sold my other car at a local used car lot, but since this one is brand new, I'm going where I can get the best deal.

"Hi, who can I talk to about selling my car? I received it as a gift but don't want it."

The woman at the front desk looks at me skeptically, and then looks out the window at where I just parked.

"The red one?" she asks.

"Yes. It's not my style," I lie. "And the person who gifted it to me refused to take it back. So, here I am."

"I can bring you to a sales associate and they can help you with a trade so you can have something you prefer."

"No, I don't want to trade," I say politely. "I want to sell it. Today. Do you not buy back cars here?"

Her brows pinch together. "We do. It's just not a request we usually get. One moment, please. Let me get someone who can help you."

I look around the dealership showroom and feel greatly out of place. I definitely didn't dress to belong, but that's nothing new for me. I don't really belong anywhere, so why try and act like I do?

"Good morning, Miss." A middle-aged man in a light grey suit greets me with his hand held out for me to shake.

"Good morning."

"I hear you're looking to sell a car you received as a gift?" he questions, and the note of suspicion in his voice isn't lost on me.

"Yes, I am. I got it yesterday, and the paperwork is in my name, but I don't want it. I was told I could do with it whatever I wanted, so I'm selling it. I need the money, not the car."

He gives me a once-over, and I keep my face neutral so I don't show my disgust. "I can help you, but I can't guarantee sticker price. Shall we go take a look?"

"Yes." I nod, and lead the way outside.

"Wow, she's a beauty. How many miles on her?"

"I think ten."

"Oh, so it's brand new."

"Yes. And while we're outside, away from the eyes and ears of your bosses, I'm looking for a cash deal. I know this is at least a hundred-thousand-dollar car and I already have an offer somewhere else. I came here to see if you can beat it."

"Smart."

"I thought so." This guy looks over at me with a grin I'm sure he uses to close deals with women all the time, but all I see is an arrogant man who is gaging how much he thinks he can get away with cheating me without being obvious about it. I just smile like I don't know his game, and stand to the side as he inspects the car.

"I can offer you seventy-five."

"Ninety," I counter, and his grin widens.

"Eighty-five."

"Ninety," I repeat, seeing if I can get him to raise.

He chuckles. "Eighty-five."

"Fine. Deal." I stick my hand out and he shakes it firmly. "I never got your name," I add, and he grins like he just won something.

"Of course. My apologies. It's Lucas."

"Cassie."

"Nice to meet you, Cassie. Shall we get the paperwork started?"

"Yes. Thank you."

I follow Lucas inside and spend the next forty-five minutes signing papers and waiting for my check.

He hands it to me and lingers for a moment before letting me take it. "I hope you buy yourself something nice with this."

Yeah, my brother's freedom. "I will."

"How about I take you out this week and you can tell me the story behind the car."

"That's sweet of you, but I can't. The guy who bought me the car probably wouldn't like it. He's a little crazy."

"Oh, uh, right, okay," he stammers, and I give him a bright smile.

"Thanks for all of your help, Lucas." I give him a wink and walk away.

He was easy.

I was able to get ten grand more than the online service was going to buy it for, so now all I need is fifteen grand to save Sean.

I take the check right to the bank and deposit it into my account for safe keeping. I can't cash it out and have that much money laying around the house. I wouldn't be able to sleep for fear someone would miraculously know I had that much cash and rob me. Or Sean would find it and gamble it all away.

On the taxi ride back to the house, I look up the club Sam told me to check out. Pandemonium.

It definitely doesn't look as nice, classy, or dare I say, *clean*, as Dark Horse. But beggars can't be choosers.

I'm dropped off in front of the house and walk down the block so I can make my phone call in peace.

"Hello?"

"Hi, is this Mitch?"

"Yes, and you are?"

"My name is Cassie. Sam, the manager of Dark Horse, said he'd contact you and put in a good word for me."

"Yes, he called. He also said you might come with some trouble."

"No. No trouble. I handled that situation. It was all a misunderstanding."

"He didn't tell me any details, but he said you're a good dancer who will bring in customers once they see you. We have enough girls tonight, and it'll be slow since it's Monday, but if you want to come in tomorrow around five or six, I'll see what you've got and we can go from there. Sound good?"

"Yes, thank you. I'll see you then."

Hanging up, I close my eyes and take a deep breath, lifting my face to the sky to feel the cold air on my bare skin.

A storm is coming. I can feel it. The sky is darkening and the air has that smell to it that brings back memories of my childhood in Boston. I love the snow. It's always been a comfort for me. It gives me an excuse to stay inside and snuggle under a blanket with a cup of hot cocoa and a slew of movies to pass the time.

I walk back to the house and call for my brother. "Sean! You want anything from the store? I need to grab some things."

He doesn't answer, so I climb the stairs and knock on his door. When we came to live with our aunt, Sean and I shared a room for a few years until I started sleeping on the pull-out couch one night, and just never went back. I didn't mind. I wanted my own space, but I wasn't going to kick my little brother out of our room.

When our aunt passed, it took me a few weeks to gain the courage to go into her room and clear her things out. But since then, I've turned her room into mine.

"Sean? Are you awake?" I ask softly through the door. I don't get an answer or hear any movement from inside, so I pop my head in. He's not here.

Shit.

Where did he go?

I quickly send him a text. I don't need him getting into any more trouble.

Me: Sean, where did you go?

Sean: Don't worry about me, Cass. I'm going to fix what I did.

Oh, no. What the hell does that mean?

Me: Please don't tell me you're gambling to try and win your debt.

Sean: I know what I'm doing, Cass.

Me: You don't. What money are you even using? Look, I got you $85,000 to give them, and I'll get the rest. Please just come home.

Sean: How the fuck did you get $85,000?

Me: It turned out that new Range Rover was mine, so I sold it this morning.

Sean: Again… What the fuck, Cass? How was that yours and you didn't know?

Me: Someone thought it was an appropriate gift and it wasn't. So, I sold it. Don't ask questions, Sean. Just get home. Now. Don't dig a bigger hole we'll never get out of. That's how we got in this mess.

Sean: Fine. I'm on my way.

I breathe a sigh of relief and collapse onto the couch.

I can't believe him. Well, maybe I can. This is who he's been for the past year and I'm only finding that out now.

CHAPTER 11
Nico

"You're still here?" my cousin, Alec, asks when I walk into his office. "I thought you'd have gone back home by now."

"Not until this thing with Cassie and her brother is resolved."

"Seriously?" he asks, surprised.

"Yes," I sigh, taking the seat in front of his desk. "She doesn't want me around, but I'm still going to be here for when she does."

"Take it from someone who waited until Tessa was in trouble and needed help...don't wait. And if you're going to have someone watching her, make sure he knows his job."

"Cassie's not the kind to ask for help. But she's also not the kind who will accept it even when she needs it."

"Sounds like someone who will keep your attention. Tessa has certainly kept mine when I didn't think any woman could."

Alec used to be such a quiet, closed-off guy. It's nice to see that Tessa is making him come out of hiding, even when I know he'd probably rather stay locked away with her and say, *to hell with the world.*

"How is she doing? How's my future niece or nephew doing?"

"She's good." He nods. "Driving me fucking crazy, but she's good. And the baby is good, too. We have an appointment tomorrow for another ultrasound, and her blood work will be in so we can know if it's a boy or girl."

"Which do you want?"

"I don't know," he says with thought, leaning back in his chair. He looks off over my shoulder at nothing in particular when he says, "I just want Tessa and the baby to be safe and healthy. But I still don't think I'm cut out to be a dad even though Tessa says I am. So, I don't know what the better option would be – boy or girl."

"Alec." I shake my head. "Man, listen to me. The fact that you even think that means you're aware of what it means to be a good or bad dad. You've got this. And you've got a good fucking woman to make sure you're a good dad. I know you're going to do everything in your power to keep Tessa and the baby safe, and give them everything they want and what you never had growing up. Vin and I don't know what you, Leo, and Luca went through with your dad when we weren't there, but I know it wasn't good. You're never going to do that shit. Am I right?"

Alec shifts in his chair, clearly uncomfortable with the intrusion on his feelings and talk of the past. "Yeah," he croaks, then clears his throat. "Thanks."

"I'm just telling you what you already knew, but needed to hear. Tessa knows who you are. She's carrying your baby, and she already married you for Christ's sake. She hasn't run after everything she's been through, and she's not going to."

Alec nods his agreement. Tessa is as deep as he is. She wouldn't leave him. And even if the thought occurred to her, Alec would do any and everything he had to in order to keep her with him.

They were the first couple I've ever seen be so completely gone for one another that the world could be burning and they'd look at each other like the other one started the fire just so they *could* be the only ones left.

It's a crazy fucking love.

A crazy fucking love that I want.

I've never wanted to burn the world for someone until I saw the flames right in front of my face, felt them in my hands, and felt the power they possess sliding through my fingers before I wrapped them around my wrist as I tried to fuck them extinguished.

But the flames prevail. Always there.

The red flames I want burning me for all fucking eternity.

"What do you need from me to help your girl?" Alec asks, getting back to why I came here.

"Her brother's name is Sean. Sean Connelly. I don't know much about him. All I know is that he used to live in New York, and then dropped off the map. He answered the door beaten and bruised on Friday when I dropped Cassie off, which is why I asked you to get a guy to watch her. I didn't want Stefano to do too much of a deep dive into her life. Just enough to know who he was. But now she's pissed at me because I looked into her at all, and won't tell me what's going on."

"You want me to ask Stef? Then you can blame me for digging into her life and you can just listen in while he works and tells me what he finds."

"Sounds like a bullshit way around it, but okay." I shrug. "I need to know if she's in trouble because of him."

Alec picks up his office phone and dials Stefano's number, then puts it on speaker. "Hey, what's up?"

"Hey, Stef, Nico's here too. I'm going to need you to do that deep dive into Cassie and her brother."

"You okay with this, Nico? You said—"

"I know what I said. Do it."

"Alright."

Stefano can find anything on anyone. He just needs a crumb and he'll find the whole fucking loaf of bread it broke off of – crumb by crumb.

I never asked if it bothers him to do this for us. We simply ask him to find someone, or dig into someone's life, and he does it. He holds all the secrets in the family because he knows all of ours. There are the favors we ask of him that no one else knows about, and the info he can find on any of us that we haven't told anyone.

He's only allowed to use his skills on us if asked or if we're in a life-or-death situation.

The phone line is quiet for a few minutes and I finish off the coffee I brought with me that's now cold.

"Oh, shit," Stefano says under his breath.

"What?" I demand, but he doesn't say anything. "What did you find?" I ask, angrier this time.

He still doesn't answer, and Alec shakes his head. "He's in the zone. He probably doesn't know that he said anything. Let him work and then he'll tell us."

"Shit," he says again, and I slam my hand down on Alec's desk.

"Stef, what the fuck did you find?"

"First, did you buy her a car?"

"What does that have to do with anything?"

"She sold a car today and deposited eighty-five grand into her account just after."

"She got more than I thought she would. Although, she does have great negotiation skills, so I should've expected that."

"You bought her a car and you're not mad she sold it?" Alec looks confused. A look he doesn't often wear.

"Yes, and yes. She said she sold her car last week which was my first indicator she needed quick cash. She wasn't going to accept my help, and I knew she was mad at me enough to not accept anything I would offer her. Especially a car. I told her to do whatever she wanted with it, and I knew she'd sell it, thinking she was getting back at me for overstepping."

"Jesus, man," Alec scoffs.

"Don't act like you didn't do dumb shit to manipulate Tessa in the beginning."

"True." He's not even sorry about it.

"I know her better than she realizes. I just don't know the big things."

"Well, you're about to," Stefano says through the phone.

CHAPTER 12

Cassie

I'm in the middle of cooking dinner when my phone vibrates on the counter.

Nico: Are you free for dinner tonight?

Is he not back in New York yet?

Me: Not for you. I'm making dinner for myself now.
Nico: What are you making?
Me: Pesto gnocchi with tomatoes, spinach, and blackened chicken.
Nico: That sounds good.

I roll my eyes.

Me: It is. That's why I'm making it.

Nico: You know what also sounds good? Me fucking that sassy attitude right out of you and then eating dinner with you. Naked.

Me: I happen to like my attitude, and I know you do too. Fucking me won't make it go away.

Nico: If it's hard enough, you'll be nice to me for a few minutes.

Me: That's presumptuous.

Nico: I'm speaking from experience, *la mia rossa piccante.*

He's said that to me before, so now that I have the written words and spelling, I look it up.

My spicy redhead.

It shouldn't make me happy that he's calling me that, but it does. The fact that there's a '*my*' in front of it...

No, I can't let myself go there.

Me: And from your experience with me, I'm spicy?

Nico: You're the perfect balance. Spicy attitude with a sweet pussy and sweet moans to go with it when I'm deep inside you.

I pop a piece of chicken in my mouth to see if it's spicy enough and start to choke when I read his message. Coughing, I gulp down some water and read it again. And again.

Nico: Got nothing to say to that, Cassandra?

Me: I told you I was cooking. I'm not waiting with bated breath for your next message to come through.

Nico: See? Spicy.

Me: **rolling my eyes**

Nico: How about I make your eyes roll back instead?

Fuck, he's too good at this. He has a dirty retort for everything.

Me: I told you it wasn't happening again.

Nico: You did. But we both know it was a lie. If I told you I was outside your house and needed your lips wrapped around my cock more than I needed my next breath, what would you say?

Me: I'd say to keep holding your breath and I'll mourn you at your funeral with my sexiest lingerie under a black trench coat in your honor.

Nico: That's evil.

Me: Only a little.

Nico: You could at least let me see you in that lingerie before you kill me. I'll take another dance, too. Then I'd die a happy man.

My heart pangs with guilt.

I don't want the reminder that he told me I only dance for him now, because that won't be true after tomorrow.

Me: You're assuming I'd take pity on you.

Nico: You're not heartless, *piccante*.

Me: No, I'm not. But I'm also not falling for your games.

Nico: No games. I'm not playing any games when it comes to you. I never have been. I'm telling you I want you and I need you. It's that simple.

The breath leaves me in a rush and I lean against the counter. He can't just say shit like that.

I put my phone down and drain the gnocchi before it gets too mushy. I add the cherry tomatoes I already roasted in the oven, pesto, heavy cream, and spinach to the cooked blackened chicken bites in the pan, and heat it up before dumping the gnocchi in and combining.

Cooking has been a comfort for me this past year. When I'm feeling out of control, lonely, or stuck, I go to the kitchen and my focus is all on the task at hand.

But right now, with Nico texting me, he's disrupting my focus. He has me picturing him sitting at the table, pouring us wine while I cook and try not to burn whatever it is I'm making because he just fucked my brains into a scramble.

Nico: I see I've said something you didn't expect. Let it sink in, Cassandra, and then text me when I can come inside. I have wine.

What?

I turn off the stove and go to the front window and look outside.

Me: You're not outside.

Nico: Not yet. I'll be there in two minutes.

Me: Why are you texting and driving?

Nico: Concerned for my safety?

Me: No. Who said I'd let you in?

Nico: You will.

Me: No, I won't.

Nico: I want to talk. That's all.

Me: I don't want to talk to you.

Nico: You already are.

Ugh!!

I toss my phone back on the counter and scoop out a portion of dinner onto two plates.

I run upstairs and knock on Sean's door. He doesn't answer, so I open the door a crack and see him sitting at the desk in the corner with his headphones on, playing video games. It reminds me of when he was younger and it was like pulling teeth to get him to stop playing and go outside for literally anything. I think he found solace in his games.

I would normally give him his privacy and he'll just come downstairs when he's hungry, but he needs to eat to gain his strength back.

"Sean." I tap his shoulder and he jumps. "Sorry!" I laugh. "I came to say dinner is ready."

"Oh, I'm starving."

"Good. Come on."

"Thanks for cooking, Cass," Sean says, taking a seat at the table. "You didn't have to do that for me."

"I'm cooking for myself anyway." I shrug. "And you need your strength to heal."

"I'll be fine."

"Mmhmm," I hum, pushing the food around my plate, avoiding eye contact. He's only going to be fine if we can come up with another fifteen grand by the end of the week.

I was lucky to catch him today before he gambled away any money he might have left.

"Where did you put the $85,000 you got from that car?" he asks casually, as if I don't see where he's going with this.

"In the bank."

"You put all that in the bank? Cassie, come on, I–"

"No," I cut him off firmly. "I don't want to hear what I know you were about to say. It's not your money to gamble with. Do you even know how lucky we were that I happen to be gifted a car like that to sell?"

"Since you brought it up... How did you get that car? Hmm? *Who* gifted it to you?" he asks cruelly, his temper flaring at me calling him out.

"What are you implying, Sean?"

"You found someone at that club pretty quickly who's willing to drop that kind of money on a car for you."

"Again," I seethe, "what are you implying?" I want to see if he has the balls to say it to my face.

"That you whored yourself out to the richest man in there."

"Shut your fucking mouth!" I spit. "I didn't and I wouldn't. How dare you." I shake my head, blinking back angry tears. "How fucking *dare* you. I only started dancing so you wouldn't be killed, you idiot!" I yell, not being able to hold back anymore.

I was hungry a few minutes ago, but now my stomach is in knots, and it drops when I see a message from Nico light up my screen.

Nico: I'm here.

I roll my eyes.
The audacity of this man.

Me: Good for you.
Nico: And for you, too, if you come to the door. Then on my face.
Me: I won't be coming on your face. Plus, my brother's here. It's really not a good time.
Nico: Good. I want to meet him.

There's a knock at the door and I freeze, my eyes wide as they dart between the door and Sean.

CHAPTER 13

Cassie

"Were you expecting someone?" Sean asks.

"No," I reply, and his eyes narrow as he looks at my phone in my hands. It's not a lie. I really didn't think Nico was going to show up.

Sean's chair scrapes against the linoleum as he pushes away from the table and stands.

"Sean, I got it. It's fine."

"Is it the guy who bought you that car? I should thank the man you used to help me."

"Don't be a dick, Sean." I chase after him, but he gets to the door first and opens it, blocking me out.

"Who are you?" he asks nastily.

"Sean–" I start, but Nico beats me to it.

"Nico Carfano," he says proudly, a dark note to his voice. He knows something's up.

Sean's eyes cut down to me. "You fucking serious, Cassie?"

Nico takes a step closer, and I can feel the controlled anger rolling off him. "Watch your mouth when you speak to her," Nico warns.

I can't take being blocked out like I need protecting. "Hey," I say sternly, and push Sean out of the way. He winces, not putting up a fight, and I don't bother apologizing because he's being an asshole. "Go upstairs. I've got this."

He looks between Nico and me, and then ultimately concedes and goes right upstairs, slamming his door like a petulant child.

I rub my forehead and sigh, then grab my jacket hanging by the door and step out onto the porch, closing the door behind me.

Now that it's just us, a calmness washes over me that I don't want to read into.

It also helps that Nico looks too good to be standing on my porch right now. He looks too good to be in this neighborhood. He looks too good in general, and I want to hate him for it, but my eyes enjoy it too much.

"What're you doing here?" I ask him, shoving my hands in my pockets as the wind gusts a frigid blast at us.

He smirks when he notices my eyes appraising him. "I told you I was coming. And look" – he holds up a bottle of wine – "I brought wine to go with dinner."

"Whose dinner? Because I didn't invite you here."

"I invited myself."

My jaw hangs open for a second and then I snap it closed. "I'm going back inside and you're leaving. Shouldn't you be back in New York already? I didn't think you'd still be here."

His eyes roam over my face. "I'm not going back just yet."

"Why? Don't you have work?"

"Nothing urgent. Besides, there's something keeping me here that I'm not ready to leave."

"Your brother?"

Nico flashes me a sexy little grin. "No, not my brother." He takes a step towards me and I stand my ground, not wanting to seem like I'm cowering away from him.

"Then what?"

"She's a who."

I lift my chin. "Then who?"

Nico lifts a single finger and lightly runs it along my jawline before taking my chin between his fingers. He brushes my lower lip with his thumb and my eyes flutter closed and open again, trying to remain strong when all I want to do is melt into a puddle at his feet.

"You, *la mia rossa piccante.*"

"I shouldn't be your reason."

"Why not? You're the only reason I need to stay." He leans in and I forget how to breathe. I forget common sense. I forget that I'm mad at him and the reason why. I forget everything.

With the way we're standing, the porch light only illuminates half his face, but I can see the need and determination written in his gaze that he means what he's saying and he wants me to believe him, too.

Nico closes the distance between us by another inch. "You're the only reason I need to stay, Cassandra," he whispers, and my brain doesn't have the chance to argue with him or call him a liar before his lips are on mine, effectively silencing every part of me that's screaming to not get in deeper with him.

His lips are soft, and it's the gentlest he's been with me.

I don't know how to be gentle. I've never had gentle.

But with each time I'm with him, Nico makes me feel like for the first time I can soften, and I won't be turned into a completely different person when I'm my most vulnerable.

He's holding back with this kiss, and I appreciate that more than he knows.

There's no rushing. There's no endgame.

Despite the flirty and dirty texts, and alpha-man insistence earlier, he still respects my words and isn't forcing more from me.

I cup his cheek and he breaks our kiss, leaning his forehead against mine. My eyes remain closed, wanting to savor everything about this moment, but I need to see his.

His deep brown eyes are waiting for me, and I feel his face muscles tick with the urge to smile when I caress his cheek.

Words fail me for the first time.

The intensity of the moment becomes overwhelming, so I pull away and take a small step back, needing a little breathing room before I'm consumed by everything about him. His eyes, face, voice, touch, smell…it's all a dizzying storm that I can't let myself be swept away in.

"Are you hungry?" I find myself asking, needing to break the silence so I'm less tense.

He gives me a smug smile that I would love to kiss off his face if I didn't just tell myself I needed a little space.

"I am."

I lead him inside, and after I take my coat off, he hands me the bottle of wine and shrugs his coat off as well. It seems like such a mundane thing, but Nico hanging his coat on the hook beside mine like he's done it a thousand times when he's come home, has my heart racing at the thought.

Nico coming home.

To Me.

It's a scary thought, and I don't know why I'm even thinking it.

I shake my head and go into the kitchen. "You can open this and I'll heat the food again." I can't bring myself to look him in the eyes yet, so I shove the bottle and opener in his hands and turn the stove back on.

Why did I invite him in here? I said I wasn't going to, but I'd be lying if I said I didn't want him here. Just being around him is settling my nerves after everything with Sean.

"I like your house. It feels lived in," Nico says in passing.

"I'm not sure that's a compliment."

"It is. I never had a home that had a homey feel to it."

"What about your place now? Isn't that a home you made for yourself?"

"It is. But it doesn't hold memories like I know this house does."

"Not all memories are good ones," I tell him, finally looking him in the eyes.

"I know," he says, a look of understanding flooding his gaze.

He doesn't know, though. No one does. I haven't told anyone everything about me. Not even Lexi. She and I have been friends going on four years now, but that doesn't mean I've spilled my life story to her. Not even when I was at my drunkest did I let my secrets slip.

I was raised to keep things to myself. *Everything stays within the family*, is what my dad always used to say. And my brother and I learned the harsh truth of what happens when you don't keep your mouth shut.

"What do you know?" I challenge.

"I know how a place that holds good memories can also be the same place that holds your worst. I know Lexi already told you who I am and who my family is, but you don't know how it was before my cousin, Leo, took over as the head of the family."

"I'd like to know. If you want to tell me, that is. I know you probably don't talk about it or aren't supposed to."

"I can. To the right person who I know I can trust."

He trusts me?

"How do you know you can trust me?" I choose to ask carefully. I don't think I've given him much reason to.

Nico's eyes remain trained on mine, never wavering in their intensity and sincerity when he says, "I know I can trust you."

"How?" It comes out as a whisper through my tight throat that's clogged with unknown feelings.

He tilts his head and his eyes narrow just the slightest. "Is there a reason I shouldn't trust you?"

I swallow hard, pushing the lump in my throat down. I shake my head and whisper, "No."

He gives me a small nod, but I see the flash of what I think is disappointment in his eyes. He casts them downward before I can get a good read.

I taste a piece of chicken to make sure it's hot enough, and then turn the stove off and dish out a portion on a plate for him before reheating mine in the microwave.

I can feel his eyes on me the entire time, and they're making me nervous. Like I'm in a fishbowl and everything is magnified rather than perfectly clear when we're so close.

"Thank you," he says graciously when we're both seated with plates in front of us.

"You're welcome." I push my food around my plate like I did before he showed up and flick my eyes between my plate and him as he takes a bite.

"Mmm," he hums, closing his eyes. "It's fucking good, Cassie."

My smile is instant. "You think so?"

"Yeah, I do." He smiles back, and I can relax as the tension wracking my body melts. He eats another forkful and washes it down with wine before his intense gaze is back on me. "The Carfano name comes with a heavy weight we all carry. Leo, Alec, and Luca – my cousins – are the sons of my uncle, Michael, who was the head of the family before Leo took over after Michael and my father were killed almost six ago."

"Oh, Nico, I'm so sorry." I swallow every unfelt feeling about my dad I've kept buried deep inside me that threatens to escape the locked part of me I caged them in when I was twelve.

"Thank you." He nods, his eyes becoming distant for a moment. "After that, the next generation stepped up so the family would have a fresh turnover and not have the older generation reporting to men half their age. It was a matter of respect, and they were willing to take a backseat to the day-to-day operations and decision making."

"What's your position?" I ask tentatively, not knowing what to expect him to say.

"I'm Leo's consultant of sorts. His right-hand man who gives him the advice he needs to hear even when he doesn't want to. The third in command you could say, with Luca being his second."

"That's an important job."

"It is," he says seriously. "We all take our jobs seriously, but we're a family first, and job titles second. Family always comes before business."

I blink away from his penetrating gaze. "That's good. Family should come first."

"Vinny lives and works here with Alec, running The Aces and our other various businesses here."

"Various businesses? That's an interesting way to allude to what you don't want to admit to."

"I can't reveal every family secret to you just yet. That would be cheating."

"Cheating?"

"You'd know everything about my family before I know anything about yours."

"Oh, right." I clear my throat. I wouldn't even know where to begin. I want to tell him. I want to share something with him. But I don't know if I can. I've kept my mouth shut like I was supposed to. Even if that world was taken from me, I still resort to the scared twelve-year-old I was who didn't know where or what my life was going to be after that day.

"We have time, Cassandra. You can tell me or not. But I'm here. I'll be here to listen."

I stare at him blankly. "You will?"

"Yes."

"But you have a life. You have a home. You have a job and responsibilities. None of which are here in Atlantic City."

"So? I made the decision the moment you got in your car and drove away last month that if I was put back in your path, then I wouldn't let you walk right past me."

"What if I turn and go back in the other direction?" I challenge.

"Then I'll follow you."

"You'd stalk me?"

"Stalking implies a stealthy operation. I'm telling you right now that I'm going to follow you, and will continue to do so, until you either turn around or I chase you down."

I don't know why, but my lips turn up in a small smile that has Nico's eyes darting between my mouth and eyes. "Okay," I finally say, and he raises his brows.

"Okay?"

"Yes. Okay."

"Okay, then." Nico and I eat in a comfortable silence for a minute, just basking in the notion that he will be here whether I try and push him away or tell him I don't want him.

He's simply going to be here.

For me.

Waiting.

No one's ever said anything anywhere remotely as beautifully crazy before, and he declared it as a simple matter-of-fact statement. As if it was such a normal thing to tell someone.

"Should I risk it and ask you to go for a drive with me tomorrow morning? I'll bring the coffee and breakfast."

"I have classes tomorrow. But not on Wednesday, if you don't mind waiting a day?"

"Of course not. So, Wednesday morning's breakfast is lined up." He winks. "But tonight's dessert?" – he rubs his jaw and wets his bottom lip with his tongue – "I can think of only one thing on the menu."

He says it while I'm taking a sip of wine and I cough into the glass, not expecting him to go there so brazenly.

"Oh," I say, feeling my cheeks heat.

I'm not a shy person by any means, but the intimacy of the night mixed with him wanting to eat me for dessert, has me blushing.

"My brother is upstairs," is all I say to deter him.

"So? I can be quiet. But wait…" He smirks, his eyes dancing with a gleam of a challenge. "I know how loud you get when my tongue is licking your pussy, so…" Nico leans back and drinks his wine like he just won something.

"I can be quiet if you have something to gag me with."

It's his turn to choke on his wine, and I just smile sweetly and flutter my eyelashes while he regains his composure.

"*La mia rossa piccante*," he rumbles low and sexy. My God, when he speaks Italian, he could literally get me to do anything for him.

"My brother is probably back to playing video games now," I add. "He wears headphones."

"Stand up," Nico commands, but I just prop my elbow on the table and place my chin in the palm of my hand while I pop a piece of gnocchi into my mouth.

His eyes narrow at my defiance, but he should've expected it.

"Stand up," he repeats, his voice carrying the authoritative undertones I'd normally cave to. I want to give in, but I also want him to know that I'm not always going to listen to him. In fact, I rarely will.

"How about you get on your knees since you're the one who wants dessert so badly."

Nico flashes me a predatory grin. It's pretty fitting considering I've felt like I'm being hunted by him. And while he's already had me at his mercy, he hasn't gone in for the kill yet.

He's circling me.

He's testing me.

He's seeing how long it'll take for me to tire before he can lead me willingly into the trap he's set for me.

"I'd get on my knees for you," I tell him. "In fact, I distinctly recall already having done so. If you ever want a repeat, then you can show me you have no problem dirtying your expensive suit for me."

"*Piccante*," he says smoothly, with an edge of amusement. "I have no problem getting any part of me dirty for you. I'd take you any way or place you'd let me."

Standing slowly, Nico loosens then slides his tie free from its knot. Approaching me, his eyes never leave mine until he circles behind me. I sit still, and he grabs each of my wrists and brings them around the chair behind my back.

"What if I want to touch you?" I ask him, turning my head to the side so it's near his as he's bent down to secure my wrists.

"I want to see how fast I can get you to come with just my mouth, and I don't want you distracting me."

"What are you going to keep me quiet with if you're already using your tie?"

"You'll see," he whispers in my ear, making me shiver with excitement.

Nico turns my chair out so my legs aren't under the table, and lifts my chin with a single finger. "You look good like this. Even better if you were naked, but still..." He smirks playfully, and I scowl, pulling at my restraint to try and break free. "It's no use. I know how to tie a knot that stays." He winks, and my anger flares.

I don't want to picture him with other women, tying them up, and fucking them so good they could pull at their restraints with all their strength and they remain tight through it all.

"Does that upset you, *piccante?*"

"No," I say through a clenched jaw, and Nico smiles triumphantly.

"Don't worry" – he leans down so his eyes are even with mine – "the thought of any other man having you like this has me thinking murderous thoughts, too."

"That's not what I was thinking," I lie.

"I see it in your eyes, Cassandra. There's no use in lying. But just so you know, I haven't had another woman since I had you. The first time," he makes sure to clarify.

"Sure you haven't," I counter, and his eyes flare.

"You think I'm lying? Am I lying when I say I've dreamt of you and your pussy every night, and had to settle for jerking off, wishing it was you. My thoughts have been consumed with you, Cassandra." Nico rubs his thumb over my bottom lip. "Your lips. Your kiss. Your scent. Your touch. Your sounds. Your voice. Your warmth. Your hair. Your sassy mouth that loves to talk back. Your insatiable need to have me that matches my own for you. *You.* All of you. Everything about you haunted me, waking and sleeping, and if I hadn't seen you Friday, I don't know how much longer I would've lasted before I showed up at your door begging for anything from you. I would've taken any crumb of attention you were willing to give me. Still am."

I'm rendered speechless.

I don't even know how to process everything he just said, let alone form a coherent answer that doesn't come out as *fuck me, please*.

"You don't have to say anything," Nico assures me, his voice soft like velvet as it caresses my racing heart to keep it from exploding. "Finally telling you is all I've thought about, and now that I have, I need to taste you again so I know you're real and this isn't just another dream."

My head nods, with every word in my vocabulary frozen in my throat while my head is screaming to tell him that it's been the same for me. That I'm just as haunted by him, day in and day out.

Nico places a soft kiss to my lips, sending a zap of electricity straight through me – setting every nerve ending on fire. I feel him everywhere. Inside of, and all over, me.

He lowers to his knees before me like a soldier or knight pledging his allegiance to his queen, and I can't wait to be worshipped like one.

Nico's hands reach for the waistband of my sweatpants and I lift my hips as he tugs them down and off me. My panties follow the same path, and the cold air hitting my wet pussy sends another shiver through me.

The way Nico looks at me… Like a hungry man who hasn't seen a meal in days, or a thirsty man who hasn't had a drop to drink while stranded in the desert.

"*Così fottutamente bella,*" he murmurs while his eyes roam all over me and settle between my thighs.

"Say it again," I urge, and he gives me a little half smile.

"*Così fottutamente bella.*"

"What does it mean?"

Nico lifts my legs up over his shoulders. "So fucking beautiful. It means, so fucking beautiful. Now, since we're not totally alone, I'm not going to waste any time getting you off. No teasing and no games."

"I think you're forgetting one thing." I pop my mouth open and Nico's eyes flare with heat again.

"I didn't forget." Nico takes my panties and brings them to his nose. He takes a deep inhale and sucks on the wet spot I already know I left there. "Mmm, a little appetizer. Now," he says, "open wide for me, *piccante.*"

I do as he says and he stuffs the cotton fabric into my mouth.

"It won't be enough to muffle anything too loud. So, I'm still going to need you to be quiet. Save your screams for when it's just us."

My answer to him is locking my ankles together around his shoulders and pressing him towards me.

He takes the hint and licks his lips, diving right into the task at hand – making me come hard and fast.

I grunt and bite down on my panties.

Why is it that when I *have* to be quiet, it seems impossible to do so? Only with Nico do I seem to not have any control over myself when we're together like this.

His hot tongue circles my clit and I squeeze my thighs around his face, which has him groaning into my pussy. The vibrations travel through me and I shake with the need for just a little more. I was already close before he even started, because apparently, I don't even need him to touch me to be turned on beyond belief. And now, I'm ready to come with just a few strokes of his tongue.

Nico slides his tongue down to my entrance and laps up the come already leaking from me before shoving his tongue inside me and sucking hard.

The chair creaks as I pull against the tie binding my wrists as my body shakes with how hard I clench my jaw and my thighs around him, trying not to make a sound.

Gripping my bare ass, Nico buries his face in my pussy, pressing his nose to my clit while his tongue is plunged inside me. With what little movement he can make with how tight I'm holding him, he shakes his head, and my already heated nerve endings send sparks off. I pinch my eyes closed and throw my head back.

Nico grunts into me, and I know he's telling me to let go by that one sound.

He doesn't want me holding back, but I'm a little afraid, not knowing if I can be quiet.

Sensing this, he grunts again and fucks me with his tongue while pressing his face harder against me and squeezing my ass.

I can't hold back.

I can't…

I…

My whole body shakes, and he all but sucks my orgasm from me with his magic mouth. And just when I'm about to let out a deep groan that I can't hold back, he reaches up and closes his hand around my throat – making sure the sound gets stuck inside.

My eyes fly open and I see white flecks dotting my vision as the greatest orgasm I've ever had rocks through me like an angry ocean beating down on the shore.

I shatter on impact, and then I'm pulled back together by the sheer force of the tides.

I don't even know how long it lasts, but when it becomes too much, and I'm deprived of oxygen for long enough, Nico releases me and I slump into the chair.

His tongue licks my pussy clean and I shudder at the continued onslaught when I'm already spent and sensitive.

Nico lowers my legs to the floor and puts my sweatpants back on me while I'm pliant and out of it. He unties my hands and takes my panties from my mouth, shoving both in his pocket.

"*Così fottutamente bella*," he whispers in my ear as he picks me up and carries me to the couch in the living room.

Nico sits with me and pulls me against him, wrapping his arm around me. My eyes fight to remain open, and ultimately lose the battle when I rest my head on his shoulder.

CHAPTER 14
Nico

"Nothing to report, Nico," Rocco says to me as I roll up to his window Wednesday morning.

"Good. Thanks, Rocco. You're relieved for the day. But be back again tonight at ten."

"Got it." He nods and pulls away from the curb while I pull into her driveway.

I've had Rocco watching over Cassie's house every night to make sure no one comes as a surprise to her or her brother. I know those he owes money to wouldn't be stupid enough to come during the day in a neighborhood like this. It's at night that no one wants to look out their windows.

I knock on her door, and when she answers a few seconds later, I take note of how tired she looks.

"I should've let you sleep longer."

"Why?" she asks, confused.

"You look tired. I'm sure you have a lot of work to do with this being your last semester."

"Are you saying I look bad?" she teases, popping her hip out with her hand on her waist.

"Never," I say quickly. "That's not what I meant. I just…you know what? Never mind." I shake my head at my own stupidity. "Are you ready? I have breakfast in the car."

"Good, I'm starving."

"I'm going to take you to my favorite spot I like to go to when I'm here."

"Okay," she says softly, grabbing her coat from the hook and her keys and small wallet from the dish on the side table to place in her pockets.

I open the passenger door for her and she gifts me with a small smile that I accept as the prize I know it to be.

For as much as I love her sassy and spicy side, I want her to feel safe to show me her soft side, too. It's the ultimate sign of trust.

"I got you a coffee. Hazelnut with a splash of cream."

"How did you…?" she starts to ask, a hint of wonder in her voice.

"I have a good memory. I listened when you ordered room service last month. And in case it ever comes up for you, I like my coffee black."

"That's easy to remember."

"But if you want to get specific, I like a really nice Ethiopian blend."

She laughs and I look over to catch her beautiful smile.

Fuck me. How is she even real?

"Okay. I'll keep that in mind," she tells me, then picks up her cup. She blows on the small opening before taking a tentative sip. "Mmm, it's good."

"It's from The Aces. I had them make us a little something for breakfast, too. Of course, if you wake up with me again in my room, then you can order as much of the coffee as you want."

"Are you trying to bribe me with the best coffee I've ever had in exchange for sex?"

"Bribery? Sex? Wow, what a dirty mind you have," I tease. "I just meant wake up with me. I never said anything about sex."

"Oh, please," she draws out, rolling her eyes. "Don't act like you're so chaste or clever."

"Alright, you caught me. I was picturing you drinking coffee in my room in nothing but a robe after a marathon night of fucking. Then your robe happens to slip open and shows me—"

"Okay," she says, cutting me off. "I get it."

I look over at her and see her hiding her smile into the lid of her cup as she continues to drink her coffee.

Damn, she's gorgeous.

I went to her Monday night to talk to her and get her to talk to me about everything I found out from Stefano. But of course, I was distracted by her right away, and my plan flew out the window. Not that I minded. I mean, Jesus, she suffocated me with her pussy and thighs, and had I died, I would've died a very happy man.

She keeps letting me do to her what comes to mind, and doesn't pause to question me. I fucking love that. She's adventurous and just as desperately horny for me as I am for her.

We drive in comfortable silence for a few minutes as we leave Atlantic City's limits and continue down towards the southern point of the island through Ventnor, Margate, and Longport.

"I've wanted to buy a house down here for a long time," I tell her as we drive along the stretch of road that borders the water.

"They're all beautiful," she says wistfully. "I've admired these houses for years. My aunt used to take Sean and I for drives and I'd daydream about living in one of these big houses on the water. I always thought life would be perfect if I did. I mean, what could be better?"

"A nice house doesn't mean a perfect life."

She sighs. "I know. It was just a daydream. I used to live in a nice house in Boston. I mean, it certainly wasn't like these, but my dad, brother, and I were happy. My mom died during childbirth with Sean when I was four, so I only remember bits and pieces of her."

"I'm so sorry, Cassie." I reach over and place my hand on her leg, and she covers it with hers.

"Thank you." She looks up at me and then back out the window. "I became a mom to Sean as we were growing up, and then after our dad was uh…" – she pauses – "died, I tried to be both parents to him."

"What about your aunt? Wasn't she there?"

"She was, I guess. She worked a lot. It's a change for anyone who was single and free to then have two kids to take care of, so I tried my best to help her, and made sure Sean and I were never too much of a burden."

"That shouldn't have been your load to bear," I tell her, and she shrugs and takes a sip of coffee.

"It is what it is. That might be why I went a little wild when I got to college. I mean, I still lived here, but Sean was older and able to stay home alone without me, which meant I got to have a little freedom for the first time."

"There's nothing wrong with that. You deserve to have fun, Cassie. Everyone does. We only have this one life, and if we don't enjoy it when we have the opportunities to, then what's the point?"

"I guess. But if I had been there for Sean more the past few years, maybe then he…" She doesn't finish her thought, but I know what she's thinking. Maybe then he wouldn't have a gambling problem.

"Maybe, what?"

"Nothing. Just, maybe he would be surer of who he is and know what he wants in life."

"He's eighteen. He has time."

"How do you–? Oh, right, you looked into me."

"Don't make it sound so sinister."

"Sinister?" She chuckles. "No, but I've never had a man look into me, so it's new."

"I'm different, is what you're saying?"

"That's one way of putting it. I can say with certainty that I've never met a man like you."

My chest swells with pride. Whether she meant it as a compliment or not, I'm going to take it as one. "Thank you."

"You really will take just about anything I say as a compliment, won't you?"

"From you? Yes, I will. Because it means I'm on your mind."

I can feel her eyes on me, and when I look over at her, I see the amusement in them despite her straight face.

"On my mind. You could say that."

"What else could you say?"

"Are we almost there?"

"Yes. Just a few minutes."

"Are we going to the point?"

"We are. I should have assumed you knew it since you've lived here for ten years."

"It's my favorite place, too," she tells me, giving me another of her soft smiles. "My brother and I used to see who could go out farther onto the jetty before the other got scared. I always won, of course. Until he got older, that is, and entered his fearless phase, while I couldn't help picturing myself slipping and getting stuck between the rocks as the waves washed over me."

"I'm glad you had that common sense."

"Yeah, but then I always owed Sean five dollars when he won." I can see her smile in the reflection of the window, but then her face falls. "That's where he got his first taste of betting, I suppose. He has a gambling problem."

"Is that why he looks the way he does?"

Cassie clears her throat. "He got into a little trouble, but I took care of it."

A little trouble? If it was a little trouble, she wouldn't have had to sell the car I got her.

"If I can do anything, let me know."

Her head whips back towards me. "I don't need help. It's a family thing and I'm going to take care of it."

"I thought you said you already did."

"Don't twist my words. You know what? This was a bad idea." She sits up in her seat and crosses her arms.

I blow out a silent breath and think of how I can salvage the morning. She just put her guard back up and firmly in place, and I don't get much time to think, because once I park at the point, she unbuckles her seatbelt and gets out.

"Cassie!" I call after her, but it gets swallowed with the wind as she slams the door.

Jesus fucking Christ, Nico. Piss her off some more. Because that's worked so well for you so far at bringing her closer to you.

Grunting, I chase after her. Damn, she's quick. She's already out on the jetty. Luckily, just a few rocks deep.

It's freezing, and the wind whips her hair all around her, making her look like an ethereal warrior surveying her kingdom before she goes to battle. The deep red against the blue backdrop is like blood in the water. And if I'm not careful, it'll be my blood.

125

Cassie has the power to cut me deep if I keep getting too far ahead of myself with her. I know she wants me, but I think she's afraid. And I understand why, I do. But she'll never understand me if she continues to keep her guard up when we're together.

Cassie also has the power to make me cut everyone who's ever cut her. I'd be her hero if she'd let me. Not the hero who saves, though. No, I'd be the avenging hero who gets rid of everyone who already has, and would dare, hurt my girl.

So, perhaps I'll be the villain with good intentions.

It's the most unlike me thing I could possibly do. I thought Leo and everyone in the family was crazy for wanting to burn the world for one single person, but I guess the view is all rose-colored from where I'm standing now, because it makes perfect fucking sense to me in this moment.

Approaching Cassie, I shove my hands in my coat pockets and plant my feet right behind her.

"You keep pushing me away," I say just loud enough for her to hear me above the wind.

"I know." She nods. Taking a deep breath, she lets it out and turns around to face me, tucking her wild strands behind her ears. "It's been engrained in me since I was a kid. Family secrets stay within the family."

"I was taught something very similar."

"I figured." Cassie's eyes hold mine, and I can see the battle she's waging on whether to tell me what I can sense she wants to finally let go of. "I don't talk about my family, Nico. To anyone. Not Lexi, who I trust implicitly, and not even my brother. It's not for lack of trying, though. I want to tell you. I've wanted to tell you a few times now, but each time it got stuck on the tip of my tongue."

"I told you I'm here." I cup her face – rubbing my thumbs back and forth across her cold cheeks. "Your secrets are my secrets, Cassandra. I want you to trust me with them, but I won't force you."

"I know. You're good like that."

The wind picks up and Cassie's chin starts to quiver. "Come on. Let's get back to the warmth of the car and we'll talk. You're freezing."

I take her hand and lead her back off the rocks and across the strip of sand until we're once again enveloped in warmth.

We both reach for our coffees, but they're lukewarm now.

"We can get fresh ones if you'd like."

"No, it's okay. Maybe later. You mentioned breakfast, though?"

"Yes." I reach back and grab the insulated bag the hotel kitchen gave me and pull out two wrapped sandwiches. "Bacon, egg, and cheese on a sesame bagel?"

"Can you read minds?"

"I wish. Then I'd get to hear all the dirty things you think about doing with me." I watch her cheeks heat and her eyes twinkle like I just caught her thinking dirty thoughts. "Are you right now?"

"No," she says too quickly. "Maybe," she corrects. "Stop looking at me like that."

"Like what?" I ask, lowering my voice to an octave I know makes her pussy wet.

"Like you are now," she huffs, stealing the sandwich from my hand and ripping it open. She takes a big bite from one half and her eyes close. "So good," she mumbles after swallowing. "Do you have any ketchup in there?"

"I do." I hold the bag out for her and she reaches in for a ramekin of ketchup to dip her sandwich in.

I start in on mine and stare out at the water, letting Cassie gather her thoughts. I know not to push her. She'll talk when she's ready.

"My dad was high-up in the McLaughlin family in Boston. I don't know the details of his position because I was still sort of young when he was killed, but I know he was important. We were never without what we needed and people seemed to both fear and respect my father wherever we went. I thought it was cool." She scoffs, shaking her head.

"He wasn't a great dad," she continues. "He had a short temper, drank a lot, and wasn't around to help with homework or show up for Sean and I when we had something that was remotely important to us. Like my dance recitals or even a single soccer game of mine or Sean's." Cassie takes another bite of her bagel. "But he tried to be more of a dad in the end, which is why he was killed. The three of us were under FBI protection at some motel outside of Boston, and when my dad and two of the agents were on their way to the FBI offices, they were all killed."

"I'm sorry, Cassie. You shouldn't have had to go through that."

"He was going to flip on the family and we were going into witness protection. It was either that or prison. He told me not to trust anyone in the McLaughlin family from that moment forward, and to never open my mouth about them either. He told me everyone knew the feds were close to making a case on the boss for one thing or another, so they planted evidence on my dad that would make him the fall guy."

Cassie wraps the other half of her sandwich up and tosses it onto the dashboard. She tucks her feet up onto the seat and covers her face with her delicate hands, then runs her fingers through her hair.

I don't dare say anything.

I don't dare correct her, either.

She has it so incredibly wrong. Her dad lied to her.

"He was just trying to keep us together," she says. "He knew we'd be alone if he went to prison and didn't want anyone else raising us. It was nice to feel like he was putting his own family first for once, and not the McLaughlins."

"I can understand that."

"I grew up surrounded by people I considered family. People who turned their backs on us without a second thought. How can that be? You can trust people with your life one day, but then cut off, kill, and abandon in the blink of an eye the next."

"Cassie." I want to say something comforting, but that's how it goes. If the boss gives an order, you follow it. Of course, Leo would never give an order like that. I don't even think his dad would've. Leo would never use someone else to save his own ass if he was caught doing something.

I don't even want to get into the fact that he would never be doing any of the dirty work himself that would cause him to have a case made on him anyhow.

"I know," she says, nodding her head, as if she heard my unspoken thoughts. "I know that's just how things are. My world was going to crumble around me no matter what, I guess. It's why I've tried to stay away from you. Not very successfully, but I tried." Cassie finally looks at me. "I know your world, Nico. I grew up in it, and I was cast out of it."

"Cassie," I say carefully. "I say this with all due respect to your late father, but me and my family aren't like the McLaughlins. We *are* a family. We have an oath. We have an understanding. We have trust. We don't plant evidence on family members so they take the fall, and we don't turn our backs on each other unless we're given an indisputable reason to."

"Nico, it's all the same. You're all the same. Money, family, loyalty, respect, blah, blah, blah. It doesn't matter if it's the Irish mob or the Italian mafia. Hell, even the Bratva or Yakuza. You're all the same."

"From the outside, it may be that simple, but it isn't. And you choosing to lump me in with people who you used to know…" I rub the bridge of my nose, needing to keep my words under control. She doesn't know what she's saying. I know we're not all the same. Angela Cicariello, Luca's girl, could tell Cassie not every family is the same, because we're nothing like the animals she used to be related to. "Do you trust me? Even a little bit?"

"What does that have to do with what I'm saying?"

"Either you trust me or you don't. What you're saying might be true to some extent, but there's one huge difference you're missing."

"And what's that?"

"I would never break your trust, Cassie. When you're with me, you're mine. You're under my protection. And with that, comes the protection of every single member of my family and every soldier in our organization. You'd be at the top of the priority list for everyone. I'd be there for you. Same goes for Lexi now that she's with Vinny. You can ask her."

"It's not protection I care about. I can take care of myself."

"You should care about it, because you have people from the McLaughlin family on your brother's back right now and I doubt you can take care of yourself against an entire family. Your brother thought he could get in with the family again, but he got in way over his head."

Cassie's shoulders sag. "You looked deeper, didn't you? Even when I said not to."

"I did. I knew you were in trouble, and you weren't telling me anything. I didn't want you getting hurt in the crossfire of whatever your brother got involved in."

"That's not your business," she says angrily, her eyes spitting fire. "You'll tell yourself anything to justify getting what you want. You were mad I wouldn't tell you everything about myself right away, so you went and found out for yourself and pretended you didn't already know." Her eyes narrow. "You knew about my mother and father already, didn't you? For how long? You let me sit here just now and tell you my closest kept secret while you pretended to not know and feigned sympathy. You're a good actor. Maybe you should switch career paths."

"Cassie, please be reasonable," I beg, and immediately know that was the wrong thing to say.

"Be reasonable?" she balks. "Are you serious? That's all you have to say?"

"No, it's not. I just don't know any other way to go about a problem. I dig into it and find a solution."

"I'm not a problem for you to fix, Nico."

"I know that."

"No, you don't. You literally just said that's how you go about a problem. My life isn't yours to sort through and solve."

Scrubbing my hands down my face, I look out at the calm water and wish that I felt the same way. Instead, I created a storm inside this car.

She's not done chewing me out, either.

"You've only known me a short time, Nico. You can't just show up and expect me to spill my life to you in a day. I've spent every night and day since meeting you, wondering about you and wishing I could know everything about you, and I hoped one day I'd get my answers. I know there's a time and place for everything, though. You know no boundaries. We've had sex, Nico. Lots of crazy hot sex that has been the best of my life, but we can't be more. I can't trust you if I'm always going to be questioning your motives and if you promise one thing to my face and go and do another behind my back."

Her words are fucking killing me. They're a hot knife moving through me, searing me in half. And the worst part is that she's right. I lied to her and she caught me.

"Cassandra–"

"Don't call me that. No one calls me that."

"You've never corrected me before."

"I am now."

She's pushing me away again.

I know she loves when I use her full name, so I know this is just her way of building that thick wall back up around herself I was finally able to crack open.

"I'm sorry I lied to you. I know my reasoning behind it doesn't make it better, but I also can't promise you I won't overstep again. I can only promise to be upfront about it."

"Take me home," she says, putting on her seatbelt and looking out the window.

Rubbing my forehead, I go through a million and one things I could say to try and fix what I broke, but I know none of them will work. She's stubborn, and getting her to open up even a little was a miracle.

I need to think. I need to be the rational Nico everyone knows me to be and find a solution that doesn't involve repeating myself until I'm blue in the face, or us yelling at each other to try and get through.

I drive her home and neither of us says anything. Cassie keeps her eyes on the world outside the window while my hands grip the steering wheel tighter than necessary as I curse myself out internally.

When I pull into her driveway, she tries to make a clean escape, but I grab her wrist when she goes to unbuckle her seatbelt.

She tries to shake me off, but freezes when I say her name. Her eyes close on a deep breath, bracing herself before she meets my eyes with a controlled veil over hers. I know that game well. She can show me nothing all she wants, but the longer I hold her gaze, the more her veil falters.

"We're not done, Cassandra. Not even a little bit. Not even close. In fact, I don't ever see myself being done with you. So, when you're thinking of all the ways you can push me all the way out of your life while trying to convince yourself I'm not the one for you, just know that I'm not going anywhere."

Her eyes drop their guard and I'm shown everything she refuses admit, and it's all I need.

I cup her face. "*A presto, la mia rossa piccante.*"

CHAPTER 15
Cassie

I close my eyes at Nico's Italian words and he drops his hands from my face and wrist.

It takes me a moment to gather my wits, then methodically unbuckle my seatbelt and climb out of the car. I was eager to jump out and leave as quickly as possible when he first parked, but now every cell in my body reluctantly follows my brain as it tells it to move farther away from him and inside the house where it's safe.

Safe.

I'm safe when I'm alone, when it's just me, and when no one is around to hurt me. Even when that comes with a loneliness that can be isolating, it's still preferable to being hurt.

I can feel Nico's eyes trained on me the entire time, and because I'm not sure about what comes next, I look back at him when I reach the front door. His heavily tinted window is rolled down halfway so I have an unobstructed view of his handsome face that's hard as stone, but marred with regret and determination.

I look longer than I should, just memorizing his face. And when I finally look away and enter the house and close the door behind me, I lean against it, exhausted. It feels like I just closed the door on what could've been the best thing to ever happen to me, but that's impossible. He can't be.

I take a deep breath and gather myself.

I've got this.

Nico was just a distraction from my current predicament anyhow, and I don't need him to interfere or make me feel bad for what I'm going to have to do to help Sean get the rest of the money.

I went to Pandemonium yesterday to audition and the manager loved me. I got weird sleezy vibes from him that I had to push down and ignore, but he said I would make a lot of money there, and that's all I care about. That's the endgame goal that's keeping me on track.

CHAPTER 16

Cassie

I wake up to a pounding headache and roll over to face away from the windows. I spent the rest of yesterday catching up on homework and readings for my classes, and then worked at the club from eight to two in the morning. I would've stayed longer, but the crowd died down and I have my two classes today. I don't need to fall asleep while the professor is lecturing.

I made a little over five hundred. Which for a Wednesday in February is pretty good, but it's nowhere near what I need. I'm not going to give up, though. I'll find a way, no matter what.

Pulling myself together, I get ready for the day, and as I'm packing my bag for school, there's a knock at the front door.

It's seven in the morning, who the hell is at my door?

If it's Nico, I swear…

But when I look through the peephole, it's not him. It's some guy in a suit, holding a big manilla envelope.

I leave the chain on the door and open it a crack. "Can I help you?"

"I have a delivery for you, Miss Connelly."

"From?"

"Mr. Carfano."

"What is it?"

"I don't know, Miss. I was told to bring it to you. That's all."

"I don't want any gifts from him, so you can bring it right back. Tell him he can't buy forgiveness." I start to close the door, but the man clears his throat.

"I don't believe it's a gift like that, Miss."

I eye him suspiciously. "I thought you didn't know what it is."

"I don't. But it feels like an envelope of papers. That's all."

"Papers?" What the hell? "Fine, give it to me." He hands me the thick envelope through the opening and I mumble a thank you as I close the door.

My name is written in cursive across the front, and I run my fingertips over the ink.

I don't have time to open it right now, but I can't leave it laying around for Sean to see. Plus, my rideshare is waiting for me out front, so I shove the package in my bag and run out the door.

I hate taking taxis everywhere I go. I really wish I didn't have to sell my car. The first one, not the massively inappropriate gift Nico bought me.

I'm surprised he didn't ask me why he didn't see it in the driveway yesterday. But then again, he probably already knew I sold it when he came to pick me up since he knows everything about me.

Arriving on campus, I make the trek to the building I need and take a seat in the back corner of the classroom. I usually like the front of the room so I can stay focused and engaged, but today I just want to blend into the back.

The manilla envelope taunts me when I pull my notebook and pen from my bag. I want to know what's inside. Why would he send me an envelope of papers?

My curiosity almost wins, and I'm about to take a peek, but the professor chooses that moment to walk in, and I shove the envelope deeper into my bag instead.

* * * *

I can't take it anymore. The curiosity is eating me alive and I can't focus on anything the professor is saying with how loud the damn envelope is calling my name.

No one took the seat beside me, so I have the whole table to myself for privacy. I pull the envelope from my bag and stare at my name again for a beat before flipping it over and unravelling the string tie holding it together.

I pull out the first piece of paper just to get an idea of what all this is, and it's a handwritten note from Nico.

Cassandra,

I know there's nothing I can say that will make what I did right, but I thought turnabout is fair play. I had my cousin Stefano put together everything he could find on me, plus a few things I thought you should know.

Read everything.

Nico

I pride myself on being a strong woman. One who can sort through the bullshit a man spews at me just to get laid.

But Nico…

I can't tell with him.

I want to believe he's genuine. He seems genuine.

It's *me* who probably seems disingenuous to him. He's given me all the indication that he wants something more with me and told me he's not going anywhere.

It was meant to take the pressure off me, but I feel the opposite. He's waiting for me to realize something I'm not sure I ever will.

I place the note back in the envelope and try my best to focus for the rest of class.

CHAPTER 17

Cassie

I can't believe him.

I can't believe what I've read and what I'm reading.

Nico gave me an entire timeline on his life, with handwritten notes in the margins. Things like where and when he was born, where he grew up, where he went to school, and it goes on.

It turns out Nico is actually a couple years older than I thought. He's thirty-two. Ten years older than me.

It feels incredibly invasive to read these things, but he's right in that turnabout is fair play. I just never expected this.

I still don't know everything he knows about me, but this gesture makes me believe he knows everything. At least,

142

almost everything. Maybe even a few of my family secrets that I don't even know.

The page I'm on is a medical record showing when he was fifteen, he broke his wrist, and on the bottom of the page, Nico wrote that it happened during a training incident.

A training incident? What does that mean?

What was he training for? And with whom?

I flip the paper over, but that's all he wrote. Pulling out another notebook from my bag, I flip to a blank page and start a list of questions to ask him when I see him again.

Oh, shit.

I just thought, *when I see him again.* I guess my brain has finally caught up with what my heart has been screaming at me since the beginning.

I've effectively pushed him away since he came back into my life, when that's all I dreamt of him doing for over a month.

I really don't know why I'm pushing him away. Nico has been chasing me, and every time I let him get close, I run in the opposite direction with the first excuse I'm given.

Although, to be fair, I think my excuses were warranted. But if I stop and think about why Nico dug into my past, rather than the fact that I just didn't want him to *know* about my past, then it's kind of sweet of him. He was worried about me and my brother, and wanted to make sure I was safe.

As I keep reading, I add more things to my questions sheet, including why he didn't want to take his father's place here in Atlantic City when he was killed, but rather let his cousin and younger brother. And on top of that, *why* was his father killed along with his uncle. Was it a rival? Is there still a threat?

Nico said the women are always protected, but have any ever been targeted or hurt? Is that why he was so adamant about telling me that?

Taking a deep breath, I look up from the papers for the first time since I opened the envelope, and look at the clock across from me in the library.

Damn it, I lost track of time, and my second class started a half hour ago. I haven't missed a class yet though, so it's not that big of a deal. Besides, these last two classes I'm taking are simply for the credits to graduate. I took summer classes every year so that I could have a lighter load at the end, and I'm extremely glad I did that. I can't imagine doing a full courseload on top of the shit I'm dealing with right now.

It's bad enough I don't know what I want to do after college. I went in undecided, and then eventually chose psychology because that's what Lexi was doing, and it meant we could take the same classes and help each other study. I guess I like it well enough. I just don't know what I want to do after I graduate.

I went to college to escape and have a little fun for once, which up until recently, my grades reflected. Only when Lexi's grandfather got hurt and she had to take a semester off this past fall to help him out, did I finally focus a little more on school since I didn't have her to rely on if I didn't understand something or needed help. Plus, I didn't have anyone to go out with anymore, so I had no choice but to study.

I already felt like I was drowning before Sean showed up on my doorstep, worrying about what I'll do after graduation and what kind of job I'll find. Or maybe I should go to grad school?

And now, if I stop too long to think, I won't be able to keep my head above water. The only time I haven't felt like that is when I've been with Nico.

I never quite feel like I'm struggling to tread water when I'm with him.

Placing the papers back inside the envelope as best I can, I pack my bag and leave. I need to think.

As soon as I'm outside, I walk around the paths until I reach the lake, and take a seat on an empty bench. It's freezing, but the cold air is waking my brain up.

The water looks beautiful. Even in the winter, with the bare trees and dead leaves covering the grass, the water glistens, winking at me.

Pulling out my phone, I dial Lexi's number. I need her to talk me through this and tell me everything's going to be okay. Or not. I need the truth.

"Hey, what's up?" she asks cheerily when she picks up. "I haven't spoken to you in like a week. That's way too long."

"That's because you're too busy fucking that man of yours to care about little old me," I joke, slipping into the fun, carefree friend she knows me to usually be.

"I'm never too busy for you, Cass."

"Are you on campus right now?"

"I just got out of class. Why? Where are you?"

"On one of the benches by the lake. Can you meet me?"

"Sure. Is everything alright?"

"We'll talk when you get here."

"Alright. See you in a few," she says, curiosity lacing her words.

I get lost looking at the water again, thinking about yesterday with Nico and how the water looked then, too. It was calm while I was a raging mess on the inside, until I felt Nico walk up behind me. Once I felt his presence, this profound sense of quietness came over me. The wind and frigid air didn't touch me, and I was still for a moment. I was present.

If I took the same moment to realize what that meant, then I wouldn't be in a constant battle with myself.

I like Nico.

I like him a little too much.

I like the way I feel when I'm around him.

He makes me feel like I'm all he sees, and I've never had that.

But how do you start something with someone who you fucked for days like you'd never see them again, then wished you would the second you left them, and when you did a month later, you were on stage in a strip club he owns...? All while you're trying to earn money to save your brother's life from the family who killed our father.

I hang my head in my hands and take a deep breath.

"Are you okay?" Lexi asks, taking a seat beside me.

"Not really," I mumble through my hands.

"What's wrong?"

"A few things. But mainly, I like Nico."

"What?" I can hear the smile in her voice when she says it and I slap her leg. "Ow, what was that for?"

"Making fun of me."

"I'm not. It's just…" she says, then pauses.

I sit back against the bench. "What?"

"I knew you did from the moment you met him. That night at Royals, you were all over him, and it looked like you two were in your own little bubble you never wanted to burst. And when he offered to give you a ride home from the hospital, you blushed. Blushed, Cassie. *You*. You never blush."

"And that's all the indication you needed to know that I like him?"

"Sure." She shrugs. "Plus, that man couldn't stop looking at you like you were his next meal."

"He is always hungry for me," I tell her, and she bursts out laughing.

"See? Vinny is the same for me. I know the look. But I'm sensing that's not the issue here."

"No, it's not. How much we want each other is not the issue."

"Then, what is? When did you start talking to him again?"

"We sort of ran into each other last weekend, and it's been…a lot since then." I want to tell Lexi about my family history, but the words are stuck on my tongue again. It's not easy. So instead, I ask her, "Has Vinny being a Carfano been something you worry about?"

"Oh." Lexi blows out a huff of air. "It was at first. I mean, I'm the one who warned you about them. But then who he is and what he does..." – she shakes her head – "it became an afterthought, I guess you could say. I realized no matter what happened, or if something did happen, Vinny would make sure I'm safe. He would save me. He would lay his life down for me to make sure I was safe."

"And that doesn't scare you? That that's even a thing to think about?"

"Of course it does," she says quickly, squinting to look out at the lake. "But it's a risk I'm willing to take. You know, I tried to fight it. Well, I think I did," she says on a laugh. "Vinny and I..." Lexi smiles. "He's worth every risk that come with being with him."

"That's what I was afraid you'd say," I tell her softly.

Lexi doesn't say anything. She loops her arm through mine and we sit in a weighted silence for a few minutes.

"I think there's more to what you're debating, Cass, but I'm not going to push you on it. Just know I love you and I'm here for you."

"Thanks, Lex." I lean my head on her shoulder.

"Should we have a girl's night tonight?"

"I can't tonight. I have to submit a paper for a class that's due by midnight and I haven't finished it." Wow, that lie flowed off my tongue smoother than I expected, and I'm a little scared at how easily it did, too. I can't tell her it's because I need to work. Then I'd have to tell her I'm dancing at a strip club and why, and I'm not getting into all of that right now. If ever.

"Okay. But we need to have one soon."

I squeeze her arm. "Agreed."

It's still the morning, and I have a long way to go until work tonight. I know exactly where I need to go beforehand.

CHAPTER 18
Nico

"Are you moving to Jersey? Why are you still there?" Leo asks when he calls.

"No, I just need more time here. I need to sort some things out with someone."

"So, a girl," he presumes. "Makes sense now."

"Does it?"

"There's not much that can keep you from work."

"I'm still handling everything from here. Do you need me for something?"

"No, Luca can handle it. I do need to talk to you about something when you get back, though. It's important. Something I want both you and Vinny present for."

The only important topic that would involve just Vinny and I is our sister, Mia.

I knew this was coming after everything with Katarina and Dante. Leo's sister was supposed to be married to Santino Antonucci as a bridging of the two families. Turned out Katarina and Dante, our family's hitter and security specialist, were in love with each other, and that arrangement was never going to work.

But my little sister?

Fuck.

Mia is going to hate it, and I don't even know if I want her to be married off to a guy whose father sold us out to the Armenians and almost got us killed.

"I can tell by your silence you probably know what it's about. We'll discuss it before decisions are made."

"Fine," I clip, keeping my emotions in check. They're already out of whack because of Cassie, and this on top of it is going to make me lose my shit if I'm not careful.

Hanging up, I toss my phone on the desk in my hotel suite and pour myself a drink. I need to regain my focus and take care of the rest of the payments to everyone in the family.

We funnel the money we get from our gambling dens around the city and monthly fight nights through a few shell companies and our legitimate companies to clean it and make it look legitimate. One of my jobs is to do payroll for each company. Our soldiers, captains, and everyone else in the family all have their names on businesses as employees, so our income is always legitimate in the eyes of the government.

Once I authorize it all, I close my laptop and pour myself another glass of whiskey.

I gave Cassie everything on me that I was willing to share on paper. Of course, I omitted my more *deadly* indiscretions that could land me in prison if anyone got ahold of the papers. Besides, if she wants to know about those, then she can ask me. I won't lie to her, but I don't think she needs details into that aspect of the family business.

A knock at the door pulls me from my thoughts, and when I answer it, I'm met with the beautiful vision of Cassandra Connelly herself.

"I got your gift," she says, holding up the envelope. "It makes me wonder what you know about me if you felt the need to give me such an in depth look into your life. But that's not what I want to talk about right now."

"It's not?"

"No." She gives a little shake of her head while wearing a sneaky little smile. "I'm here because I'm tired of denying what I want."

"And what is it you want?" I ask smoothly, darting my eyes between hers. I don't want to miss anything.

"You. This. Us." Her words hit me right in my heart and I'm fucking soaring. "I don't have all the answers," she continues nervously, "and I still have a lot of questions. But what I do know, is that I'm tired of fighting with myself when it comes to you, and I just want to have one thing that's all mine."

"And that's me?" I probe, needing her to say the words. I don't want any more hot and cold. I want to hear her say it so there's no doubts.

"Yes, that's you," she says confidently.

"It's not that easy now," I tell her, and she narrows her eyes.

"What do you mean?"

"I've been nothing but open with you and how much I want you, Cassandra." Her eyes flutter at my use of her full name. "Now *you* need to show me how much you want me."

I step back to let her in my room and her eyes flash with that spicy need to fire back at me, but she bites her tongue.

I take a seat in the club chair I have positioned to face the windows, beckoning her over with the wave of two fingers.

Cassie walks around me to stand in front of me, and I swirl my whiskey in my glass. "Get on your knees, *la mia rossa piccante*. I don't need you to say anything to know you want me. Your mouth has a much better way of apologizing that doesn't include words."

Cassie raises her chin. "I never said I was apologizing."

I tilt my head. "Then why are you here?"

She remains silent.

"You're tired of pushing me away," I tell her. "So pull me closer, *piccante*. Right into that hot little mouth of yours."

I can see her need to talk back, but she rolls her lips between her teeth to hold back, making me smile. That stuns her, and my smile widens. The list of things in my arsenal to get Cassie to turn to putty in my hands is growing.

Cassie takes her coat off and folds it over the back of the couch. She starts to kneel, until I hold up my pointer finger to stop her. "Wait. I want you naked first. I want to see what's mine."

She unzips her heeled boots first, then slowly peels her skin-tight jeans down her legs. The determined set of her jaw and fiery passion in her eyes has my cock rock-fucking-solid.

She takes directions so well when she has something to prove.

Cassie lifts her sweater over her head and drops it to the floor at her feet. She stands before me in black panties and a purple bra that looks so damn good against her skin and red hair.

She reaches behind her and unclasps her bra. When the satin falls away, I'm greeted to her perfect tits and nipples that are begging to be sucked, pinched, and pulled so they turn that deep red shade of her hair I fucking love.

I rub my bottom lip to keep from reaching out and touching her, and scrape my teeth over my bottom lip when she shimmies her hips and pushes her panties down. Cassie stands proud in front of me with her shoulders back, jaw set, and eyes ablaze. A goddess.

I swirl my finger in the air. "Turn. Let me see all of you."

She obliges, and when she's back facing me, I grab her by her inner thigh and pull her towards me. She braces herself on my shoulders and I waste no time sliding my hand up to cup her pussy.

Fuck, she's already drenched.

"You like when I tell you what to do." It's not a question. I already have the answer coating my fingers.

When Cassie doesn't say anything, I slide a finger inside her, and she chokes on a little moan.

"Once I get my apology, you'll get yours, Cassandra."

"You already apologized," she says, dazed by my touch. "The envelope."

"Oh, *piccante*," I tease, stroking her slowly. "That wasn't my apology. That was what you deserved. My apology will come in the form of your come. All over my hand, on my tongue, coating my cock. All night long."

"Ohh," she sighs, tilting her hips towards me, trying to get more from me.

I take my hand away and bring it to my lips. "Mmm," I hum, "the best appetizer there is."

Cassie watches me clean my finger off and her pupils dilate. She slides her hands from my shoulders, down my chest and thighs, and braces herself there as she lowers herself to her knees between mine.

She runs her hands back up my thighs and traces my cock through the fabric of my pants. The gleam in her eyes tells me she's going to torture me a little before she gives me what I want. My own punishment for having her make me come before she does.

What she doesn't know is how many times I wished for this moment this past month. She can tease me as much as she likes. At least it's real. At least she's here. And I'm going to come down her throat no matter what.

Cassie adds pressure to her touch, making me so fucking hard, I have to concentrate not to come in my pants like a damned teenager.

I grip her wrist to stop her movements. "Is something wrong?" she asks sweetly, her false innocence turning me on even more.

"Yes," I grunt. "My cock should be hitting the back of your throat right now, but you're insisting on being a little tease."

Cassie bites her lip and I growl. I know what she's waiting for.

"Take my cock out. Now."

Her eyes twinkle with approval and her hands go to the fly of my pants, making quick work of the button and zipper. Reaching inside, I groan when her hand wraps around my cock and pulls it out – freeing me from the tight confines.

Fucking finally.

"Squeeze me," I demand, and her gentle grip tightens. "Now give me your best, Cassandra."

She licks her lips and holds my gaze as her head lowers. The pretty pink tip of her tongue peeks out and rims the tip of my cock.

I suck in a breath through clenched teeth and my muscles seize.

Fuck me.

I can't handle any more teasing.

"Suck me off. Now."

Cassie looks up at me, and with a small lift of her lips as the only warning I'll get, she takes as much of me in her hot little mouth as she can take – all at once.

"Fuck," I grunt, gripping the arms of the chair.

She squeezes the base of my cock and sucks me hard, swirling her tongue around the head when she comes back up.

I reach for her nipple and tweak it, making her whimper and moan, and the vibration shoots straight through me.

Cassie starts out slow, but I need more. "Faster," I order, and her eyes slice to mine.

My God, she's fucking beautiful.

Her lips stretched around my cock, her eyes mad and wild, and her naked body flushed with the enjoyment of taking my orders. All of it is fucking beautiful.

Watching my cock disappear in and out of her mouth brings the fire licking down my spine quicker than I'd like. I want to hold out and prolong this vision and feeling, but my need to shoot my load down her throat is greater.

"Take more," I hiss out, sliding my hand into her hair and gripping her roots at the back of her head.

Cassie hums around me and relaxes her jaw to take me all the way to the back of her throat. I grip her hair harder and hold her there for a few seconds before pulling her up.

Her gaze is watery, but filled with determination. She wants to give me what I want and what I need, and what I need is to fuck her mouth.

Controlling her movements now, I guide her up and down my cock, quickening the pace and grunting every time I hit the back of her throat.

"Fuck," I groan. "You're going to swallow everything, *piccante*. Don't waste a single drop of my come you've earned."

Cassie moans her approval and doesn't resist me.

I stiffen even more and she squeezes my base, cups my balls, and sucks me like a fucking vacuum to pull my orgasm from me like she's as desperate for my come as I am to fill her with it.

"Fuuucckkk," I groan, long and low, holding her down on my cock as my come shoots down her throat.

Cassie hums as she swallows around me – taking it all.

I loosen my grip on her and she ascends my length, licking me clean as she goes.

Sitting back on her heels, she swipes the corners of her mouth with her thumb and licks it clean as well.

Jesus fucking Christ, she's going to kill me.

"Did sucking my cock turn you on, *la mia rossa piccante?*"

She runs her hands through her hair – her tits lifting in the process – and gives me a little nod.

"Let me see."

Cassie's hand drifts down between her legs and swipes her finger through her pussy, holding her glistening finger up for me to see.

I grab her wrist and haul her up off the floor. I bring her finger to my lips to get a little taste of my lunch.

I pull on her arm so she falls against me, and I slam my lips against hers. She softens immediately and kisses me back with a hunger for more.

"It's my turn now," I murmur against her lips, and slip my fingers right inside of her with ease. She's so damn wet. So damn ready. So damn perfect.

CHAPTER 19

Cassie

Nico plants kisses down my spine and I hum my approval. His fingertip traces the shamrock tattoo on my upper right butt cheek I got when I turned eighteen and was in my rebellious, party, let loose phase of college. I was feeling a little nostalgic for my life in Boston and what could have been.

"Luck of the Irish," he whispers, his warm breath tickling my skin right before his lips meet my tattoo in a soft kiss.

"Not always lucky," I whisper back. "But I feel lucky right now," I add, and Nico caresses the globe of my cheek lovingly.

"I'm not Irish, *piccante*, but I'm the luckiest motherfucker in the world to have you. To talk to you. To touch you. To kiss you. To be able to do this," he says, sliding his hand between my thighs to tease me.

My back arches towards him automatically, but he slides his hand away to trace my other tattoo on the back of my upper left thigh.

"What does this say? I never got to ask you." His fingertip follows the Gaelic script.

"Love is the whole thing. We are only pieces."

His finger pauses its movements and he kisses the words before resuming his tracing.

My eyes sting with a rush of emotions I wasn't expecting, and I blink them back.

"I've never told anyone what it means before or why I got it," I admit, his soft touch lulling me into a relaxed state. "I got it a couple years ago as a reminder to myself. It's a part of a poem by Rumi. We're all just pieces to a puzzle, continuously looking for other pieces to fit with us to make us whole. People to love, what brings us joy, where we belong. It all comes together to be a picture of love."

"I like that," Nico says softly, kissing my tattoo again. "You just described how I feel about you perfectly."

"How?"

"A piece of my puzzle that's been missing. You fit just right, Cassandra."

I pinch my eyes closed to keep the unshed tears from escaping. That's the nicest thing anyone's ever said to me.

"I feel the same way," I admit, and a large chunk of the wall I've kept my heart barricaded behind is demolished.

Nico rolls me onto my other side so I'm facing him, and he tucks my wayward hair behind my ear. He's looking at me with soft brown eyes. Open brown eyes that have me feeling like warm chocolate is flowing through my veins rather than blood.

"What made you need that reminder?" he asks gently. He wants me to open myself even more for him, and for once, I want to share something I've never talked about.

"It's a story a few years in the making."

Nico cups my cheek. "I'm not going anywhere."

I lift my chin and give him a quick kiss before tucking myself against him. I can't look at him when I tell him this. Not that I'm ashamed. I just don't talk about myself, and I'm already feeling too vulnerable.

"At the end of my freshman year of college, Lexi and I went to a frat party to celebrate the end of finals week. I got a little too drunk, and when I went to find the bathroom, I was followed. I was too wasted to know what was really happening, and was lucky Lexi came looking for me when she realized I wandered off alone. She saved me. She pushed him off me before he could do anything and then got me out of there."

Nico doesn't say anything. He just drags his fingers up and down my spine, so I keep going.

"I woke up the next day extremely grateful. I know it wasn't my fault. It was his for trying to take advantage of me. But I made a promise to myself that I was going to be more careful with myself and the situations I put myself in. Rumors spread about me through the frats that I was down for anything and up for the taking because I dated one for a month and had a one-night-stand with two others. They needed to save their egos by making me sound easy rather than admit I wanted nothing more from them. I got the tattoo a year later to remind myself that there's more out there for me.

"I only started to try dating recently because I was tired of being alone, but it was a disaster. No one was interesting. No one made me feel like they were listening to me when I talked. And" – I reach up and trace his jawbone – "no one made me feel anything like how I do right now. Not even close. In fact, I felt nothing until you."

Nico lifts my chin to look into my eyes when he says, "You were looking for your lost puzzle piece."

"Yes," I whisper, and his lips are on mine in an instant.

He kisses me with a passion I haven't gotten yet. This is different. This is a silent agreement between us that we're both feeling the same thing. We're both realizing that this is real and there's no more confusion for either of us.

Nico rolls on top of me and I slice my fingers through his hair, holding him to me.

"Cassie," he says roughly against my lips, pressing his forehead to mine. "I want to feel you. I want this moment to keep going. I want to be as close to you as possible."

"I've never done that."

"Me either. I've never wanted to be so close to someone before you, Cassie."

I stare into his eyes and see nothing but the truth shining in them. He's going to make my heart explode with too many emotions I'm not used to if he keeps saying such sweet fucking things.

"I'm on the pill," I tell him. "I...I want to feel you too, Nico." I scratch the back of his head, which elicits a low rumble from the back of his throat. "I want you to be the one I'm closest to."

"*Piccante*," he cajoles, and my lips lift in a small smile.

"Not so *piccante* right now. I'm agreeing with you."

"You know I like you both ways." He kisses me hard, pressing me into the bed with his full body weight.

I hook my legs around his hips and tilt mine up so he can easily position himself at my entrance.

I don't know why I'm nervous, but I am. I have butterflies in my stomach like it's my first time all over again. Except this time, it's with a man I actually like and a man who I think is worthy of taking this first from me.

"Look at me, Cassandra," Nico urges. "Let me see those pretty blue eyes when I feel the tight, wet, heat of your pussy envelope me in the best fucking hug I'll ever get."

I meet his warm brown eyes again, and he slides right into me.

My neck arches back and I bite my lip, but I keep my eyes on his. His gaze feels like a warm hug of my own, covering me in his protection and love.

Yes, love.

I see it and I feel it.

I don't care how long it's been. Or rather, how long it hasn't been between us. This is how I want to feel for the rest of my life. This is how I want to be worshipped for the rest of my life.

"Me too, *piccante*. Me too."

My eyes tear up and he kisses me while he fucks me slow and easy until the pressure in me builds to where I may explode or I may beg him to never stop. I can't decide because I can't think straight.

"Come for me, Cassandra. Let me feel your pussy squeeze me before I fuck you hard and fast like we both like."

"Please," I whisper, and Nico smiles as I let go.

"Fuck, baby," he groans, kissing the corner of my mouth. "You feel so good."

"You too," I manage to choke out, and his smile grows. My God, he's gorgeous.

Nico nips at my chin and buries his face in my neck, only to lick his way up to my ear and take my lobe between his teeth.

"Nico," I groan.

"Just what I wanted to hear," he says, then fucks me like he hasn't before.

It's rough, raw, and fueled by the chase of needing to prove something.

"Keep your eyes on me," he demands. "I want to see how I make you feel."

I already feel too exposed, and now he wants to see more. He wants to see it all. I try and look away, but I can't. I want to see how I make him feel just as badly, and what I see has me ready to explode.

"Come for me again, Cassandra."

I dig my heels into his ass. "Harder," I say between thrusts. "A little" – I gasp – "more."

Nico grunts and his eyes darken with my request. He grips me behind my knees and presses my legs forward, opening me wider and taking away my control as he fucks me harder.

He hits a new spot in me, and after only a few strokes, I'm a goner. My inner muscles flutter around him and then seize.

I...

My throat closes around a scream.

No sound. Just my mouth open as my body falls apart and my heart swells.

I didn't know sex could feel like this.

I'm on fire while I'm drowning, and my next breath only comes when Nico's lips crash against mine and he breathes life into me.

Nico pumps through my orgasm and then stills, groaning into our kiss as he finds his own release.

Knowing he's filling me with his come sets off another orgasm, and I tear my lips away from his to finally find my voice with a gasp and then long moan.

"*Così fottutamente bella,*" Nico whispers in my ear as he pulls out.

I whimper at the loss and feel our mixture of releases leak out of me as he rolls us over so I'm lying on top of him.

I rest my head on his chest, and his rapid heartbeat makes me smile as I drift off, feeling safe and happy in his embrace.

CHAPTER 20
Nico

I stroke Cassie's hair while she's fast asleep on top of me. She's making this cute little snoring sound she hasn't before, and I take it as a sign I fucked her into a deep sleep that has her comfortable in my arms.

She showed me how she felt. I didn't need the words.

With how guarded she's been, I can guess she didn't want to show me she really is deep in this with me like I am with her.

"Mmm," she hums, squirming on top of me.

I twirl the ends of her hair with one hand and palm one of her perfect ass cheeks with the other. I press the pads of my fingers into her flesh, which elicits another squirm of her hips against mine.

"*Piccante*," I say, more to myself than her, and she hums again. Yeah, that sound is only making my cock harder.

I think my girl needs a wakeup call.

I lift her hips and position myself so I can slide her right down my length in one motion.

Her eyes fly open and her pussy squeezes me like a fucking vice.

"Fuck," I grunt, while Cassie moans, digging her nails into my chest.

"Nico," she says, in that breathy moan I love.

"Ride me, baby. I want to see your tits jiggle as you bounce on my dick."

She rolls her neck back and braces herself on my chest, ready to give me a show.

I keep my hands on her hips, controlling her movements at first. But when Cassie's eyes glaze over and she bites her lip, I let her take the lead. I want her to use me for her pleasure, and I want to watch her as she does.

She's amazing.

She always unabashedly takes and gives me everything, every time, and it's a beautiful fucking sight.

She's a beautiful fucking sight no matter what she's doing. But when she's taking my cock like this? Fuck me, I've never seen anything more beautiful.

"I'm almost…" she moans, bouncing on my dick and then rolling her hips. "I need…" She gasps and shudders when my thumb presses against her clit. "Yes," she hisses, a smile tilting her lips up and her eyes finding mine again – wild and untamed. "Come with me, Nico."

"I'm with you, *piccante*." And I am. Cassie lifts up, her pussy clenched around me so hard, it's like she's trying to pull my goddam soul out of me. Until she drops down onto me, making us both groan on impact.

"Again," I tell her, and she smiles down at me, repeating the move and adding two short bounces. "Cassandra," I croon, rubbing circles around her clit.

"Nico," she croons right back in a sweet voice I want to record so I can listen to it on repeat whenever she's not with me.

Rocking her hips, she does the move one more time, and on her descent, I press on her clit and pinch her nipple, making her scream as her orgasm rips through her. Her greedy pussy milks my cock in waves, pulling my orgasm from me so I can fill her up.

Cassie collapses on top of me and I wrap my arms around her.

When we catch our breath, Cassie mumbles against my neck, "I'm hungry. And thirsty."

"What do you feel like having?"

"A big, fat, juicy BBQ bacon cheeseburger with fries and a diet coke."

That makes me chuckle. "I like a girl who knows what she wants. You rest, and I'll order us food."

"Can you also bring me some water?"

"Yes, my queen," I say, and she slaps my ass as I'm getting out of bed.

"Keep up the compliments and I'll make you my king."

I cup her face and plant a kiss to her swollen lips. "That's the plan, *la mia rossa piccante*."

* * * *

"Can I ask you a few questions about the envelope you gave me?" Cassie asks me over lunch.

"Of course. I figured you would have some. I'll answer anything honestly, but I can't guarantee you'll like the answers."

"That's fair."

"Then ask whatever you'd like."

"I saw you broke your arm when you were a teenager and you wrote it happened during training." I nod my head. "What were you training for?"

I pop a fry in my mouth and take a moment to think on how I want to phrase this. "I told you I grew up in the city away from my dad because he wanted his kids to grow up and go to school with our cousins. But it was also so we could train together. My uncle was very meticulous and always assumed the worst. He trained his sons and nephews like we were going to go to battle with a rival family at any given moment. It's been useful, but it was a fucked-up way to be raised."

"Have you ever had to do that? Go to battle with a family?"

"That's a story for another time," I tell her, not wanting to get into the dynamics of the families right now – Italian or otherwise.

"So, how did you break your wrist?"

"We were practicing Krav Maga and I was facing off with my cousin, Leo, when he was able to get a good grip on me while we were grappling. The next thing I know, I hear the crunching of my wrist."

"Oh," she says, her eyes widening all cute in surprise.

"It wasn't my dominant hand luckily, but it gave me the opportunity to learn how to accurately shoot one-handed and throw a knife pretty well."

"Oh, okay. Well, there's a positive, I guess," she says sarcastically, rolling her eyes.

"Every negative situation, even painful ones, can have a positive side result," I tell her, and her eyes dart to mine and then away quickly.

She clears her throat. "That's true," she says, then changes the subject back to me. "I have more questions, though."

"Alright." I nod. "I'm ready."

"Why didn't you take your father's position here in Atlantic City? You let your cousin and little brother instead."

"I didn't want the job," I tell her honestly. "I preferred the city at that point, and Vinny and Alec were the ones who loved AC and running their own operation here. However," I add, "if I knew you were here, then I would've made a different choice."

"No." She shakes her head. "Everything happens for a reason. We met when we were supposed to. If I met you sooner, I wouldn't have known how to handle you."

"Handle me?" I can't help but smile. "You know how to handle me, *piccante*? Because I still don't know how to handle you, and I don't want to know. I like not knowing if I'll get spicy or sweet Cassandra."

She smiles and takes a bite of her burger. "I don't really know how to handle you," she admits after swallowing. "But I don't really want to handle you either. Just understand you."

"Not much to understand."

"I don't believe that."

"I value family, honesty, and loyalty more than anything else."

"I agree," Cassie says, and we share a silent moment with our eyes locked. It's one where we say more than what was said.

"Any other questions?"

"I have one more. But to be fair, I didn't get through the entire envelope. Only until your father's death."

"Why?"

"It was a lot for one sitting. Going through 32 years of someone's life isn't exactly light reading. I didn't realize you were so old."

"Old?" I choke out. Cassie looks at me all innocent, but then smiles and laughs. "You think I'm old?"

She shakes her head and eats another fry. "No. You're ten years older than me, though. You don't think I'm too young for you?"

"Not at all. Am I too old for you?"

"Not at all," she says, a little smile dancing on her lips.

"And I may be older, but I have as much experience with a serious relationship as you do."

"So, none?" she asks, the hope in her eyes making me glad I never gave another woman a chance.

"You're correct," I confirm, and the hope in her eyes turns to happiness. "I don't date, Cassie. I don't get possessive over a woman and not want anyone else to see her the way I do. A woman has never made me want to murder a room full of people before. Aside from my family, of course. I've never shared my life with a woman or handed them an envelope of my secrets. I've never had a woman consume my every thought, waking and sleeping, from the moment I met her before. I've never before felt the way I do right now, Cassandra."

"Nico." Cassie blinks rapidly and I see the glassiness to them she's trying to hide.

"Come here." I push my chair back and tap my leg. Cassie stands and scurries over to me, and climbs onto my lap. I run my hands up and down her back. "All we need to do is feel what's right. That's how we'll navigate what's new for the both of us. Okay?"

"Okay," she says softly, sealing the deal with a kiss equally as soft, but still manages to rock my world off its axis.

I stand with her in my arms and walk us back to the bed. I think she's finally starting to realize how deeply she's planted herself into me, and I'll keep telling her every chance I get until she believes it without a doubt.

CHAPTER 21

Cassie

Carefully and quietly, I sneak out of bed and into the bathroom. After sorting myself out and forcing my hair to look at least semi-tamed, I tiptoe back out and look at Nico fast asleep in bed.

He looks relaxed and at peace, and I'd like nothing more than to slide right back into bed with him, but I can't.

I leave him there and walk out into the living room of the suite to get dressed where I left my clothes earlier.

Nico knows I love when he orders me around and takes control, and I love that I never had to tell him that. He could read it from me right away.

Sneaking out is not what I want to do, but I also don't want to tell Nico I can't stay because I have to work tonight. He doesn't know I found another job, and I know by his reaction the first time he saw me at Dark Horse, he's not going to like that I'm still dancing. Especially after today.

I don't want to do it at this point, but it's a necessary means to an end. I don't even know what I'll say to Nico when he asks me why I snuck out, but I need to think of my brother and getting him out from under the McLaughlins' thumb. Tomorrow is the deadline, and I need as much money as I can scrounge up to buy a little more time until I can get the full amount.

I have to compartmentalize my priorities.

Nico will have to understand when I explain things to him, and I hope he does. He'll probably just tell me I should've asked him for the money, but I don't have that in me. I'd never do that. I know he's used to solving his family's problems, but this is *my* family's business, not his.

I slept longer than I meant to after Nico gave me my sixth, or maybe seventh, or tenth, orgasm of the afternoon. I lost count. And if I didn't have to work, I would be ready to go a few more rounds with him.

Heading back to the house, I have just enough time to shower, change, dry my hair, and heat up some leftovers to scarf down before my taxi arrives to take me to Pandemonium.

When I'm up on stage, I think about Nico. It makes it easier to imagine it's just him sitting in front of me and not a bunch of strangers ogling me.

After my first stage appearance, the manager catches me on my way back to the dressing room. "Hey, Cassie?"

"Yeah?"

"I have an offer for a VIP session with you."

"What do you mean?" I ask nervously.

"A client wants a private dance from you in one of our VIP rooms in the back." He nods his head to the back of the club where a bodyguard stands in front of a hallway with a velvet rope.

"No." I don't even have to think about it.

"You can make some real money back there, Cassie."

I look up at him. "No." I don't even need to think twice about it.

"Alright," he concedes, shrugging his shoulders. "Let me know if you change your mind." He releases my arm and I scurry into the locker room.

A private dance. Sure.

* * * *

Counting my money, I take fifty off the top and leave it for the house mom. Another dancer told me she makes the schedule, and when I asked her what I had to do to not get day shifts as the newbie, she just looked at me like I was dense. So, I gave her an extra fifty last night on top of the fifty I was already giving her to put me on nights. I do the same tonight.

Honestly, I think I'd be pretty good at that job. Making sure the girls are safe, treated fairly, and well fed and hydrated throughout their shifts. I love watching the women perform, so I think it'd be fun to help hire them, too. Or even help in giving lessons and making routines.

Packing my bag, I order a taxi and wait until it's here before I go out the side door and right into the back seat. I know this neighborhood and I know not to stand around alone outside a strip club with a bag full of cash. I don't need any more trouble than I already have.

The driver pulls up to the house at around three thirty, and I hurry inside.

"Cassie."

"Oh my God!" I gasp, my hand going right to my chest. "Sean, you scared me! What the hell are you doing awake?"

"Waiting for you," he says.

"Okay? And you need to be sitting on the couch in the dark and silence so you scare me half to death?"

"No, I fell asleep." He rubs the back of his neck. "They called and set the meet for the money later today."

"Okay, I'm coming with you."

"What? Cass, no. Not happening."

"The only way they can get their money is through me, Sean. I'm the only one who can transfer it to them."

"Just give it to me and I'll handle it. Or, do you not trust me?"

"Jesus, Sean, trust you? After everything that's happened? I had to stop you from gambling away what little money you might have left just a few days ago. I trust you with my life, but not my money. I'm going with you. No arguments." He never actually apologized for the shit he said to me on Monday, either. I gave him a pass because of what's going on, but it would've been nice to hear all the same. So, give him access to my account or a duffel of cash? Nope. Not happening.

"Fine. Whatever," he concedes. "We're meeting them at noon."

"Where?"

"Their pub in the city."

"Great. We have to pay for a car to get there now, too. Alright," I sigh, "we'll leave at 9. I don't want to be late."

I go upstairs and shower and get ready for bed, but when I lay down, I'm not tired in the least. I've never been able to sleep when I'm stressed.

I stare at the ceiling and grab my phone. I saw Nico had texted me when I was at the club, but I didn't want to open the messages yet. I couldn't.

Nico: I woke up to an empty bed. Where did you go?

Nico: I had plans for you, *la mia rossa piccante.*

He leaves it at that, but messages again a few hours later when I don't answer.

Nico: Just want to make sure you're okay, Cassie. Let me know when you get this.

I release a rush of air and throw my arm over my eyes. I'll have to message him in the morning, but I don't know what I'm going to say.

I can't tell him the truth, while at the same time, I don't want to lie to him.

It turns out I don't need to worry about which I'll do, because when my phone pings with a new message, my stomach drops and my heart twists.

CHAPTER 22
Nico

"Is she home?" I ask Rocco as soon as I answer his call. I've been waiting for an update for fucking hours now.

"Yeah, she just got here in a taxi."

"Did she look okay?"

"I didn't see anything wrong. She got out and hurried right inside. She had what looked like a gym bag with her."

"Follow the driver and ask him where he picked her up from."

"On it. I'll call you back."

I don't want to think about why she left me after everything we shared today and why she's getting home at three fucking thirty in the morning, because I'm pretty sure I can take a good guess.

I pace the living room of the suite and right over to the desk to pour myself a hefty glass of whiskey. I gulp it down and stand in front of the windows, looking down at the boardwalk.

I thought there was something wrong. I thought I did or said something that was too much for her and she ran. Cassie is the most unpredictable woman I've ever met.

My phone rings again, and I answer it quickly. "Where did she come from?"

Rocco hesitates to answer, but ultimately says regretfully, "Pandemonium."

I hang up on him.

Fuck!

I fucking knew it.

How could she?

She got a job at another strip club. And Pandemonium? Jesus, that place is fucking sleezy. She came to me today. She came to me and said I was what she wanted.

And after what we shared today?

Then she sneaks out and goes to work at that fucking place? Showing her body to men who don't have the right to even breathe the same air as her on this earth, let alone see her fucking naked.

She played me.

I'm fucking fuming, and I don't know what do with my anger. This is new for me. I'm not an angry person.

Breathe in. Breathe out.

I take a few deep breaths and pour some more whiskey before I'm even a little bit calmer.

I told her she was only going to dance for me, but I should've known her stubborn ass would find another club to work in rather than ask me for help.

I mean, Jesus, how much money does she fucking need to help her brother?

I gave her a car to sell and it still wasn't enough?

She sure as shit wasn't acting stressed over money today. I thought we were good.

Goddamn it, why didn't I ask her?

Probably because I was loving how open she was for the first time that I assumed everything was good.

Well, since I know she's awake, I'll send her another message.

Me: What part of you only dance for me now did you not understand, Cassandra?

She doesn't answer me straight away, so I try again, letting the whiskey I'm drinking get the better of me.

Me: I didn't realize you needed more money than the car I gave you that you sold. I would've given you more for the performance you gave me today if I knew.

Cassie: Did you really just say that? Fuck you.

Me: You already did.

Cassie: I'm doing what I have to to save my brother.

Me: I could've helped, but you're too proud to ask for help. You'd rather take your clothes off and have strangers shove money in your tits and ass rather than have someone who cares about you help you.

Cassie: You don't get to say that to me. I never asked you to care about me, and you don't get to judge me for my choices when I know what you've done for your family. You think I haven't overlooked fucking a killer?

I throw my phone onto the couch. Did I imagine today? Did I create a whole fucking fantasy between us where we were on the same page and basically confessing our love for one another?

Am I fucking crazy? Did I imagine all that?

Standing, I eat up the distance to my room in angry strides to pack my shit up. I need to go home.

This is why I don't get attached to anyone.

This is why I don't fuck women more than once.

Cassandra fucking Connelly got under my skin and now I don't know what to do.

It turns out I was right to not trust or let myself care about a woman. It fucks you over. *They* fuck you over.

In the family, I'm trusted to remain impartial and be able to give advice and make decisions that are best for everyone. And yet this woman has my brain and the stupid organ in my chest at war with each other, and I don't know what's good for me.

My head is telling me to go back to the city and back to work, but my heart doesn't want to leave her.

I want her to want me.

I want Cassie to choose me.

And I know I'm an asshole for even thinking that because she's doing it to help the only family she has left, but I get to be an asshole if I want to be one. Especially when I have the means and am able to help her however she needs.

I thought we worked through me having her fired.

She's a good fucking actress if she can be with me and make me believe she's finally going to be all in with me while knowing she's about to go take her clothes off for other men the second she can get away from me.

She said she's overlooked me being a killer, but I don't even know how those two things compare. I've killed those who've deserved it. Men who have brought nothing but evil into the world since they took their first breath. I did the world a few favors ridding it of them. Cassie could ask me about them and I would tell her the same.

I shove all my shit into my bags and get the fuck out of the room. I see her everywhere in here, and there's no way I'm getting any sleep in the bed that still has her scent clinging to the sheets.

I ride the elevator down to the ground floor and switch to another, private one, that will give me access to our family's level in the parking garage. I have to punch in a special code, give my fingerprint, and have my retina scanned for it to descend.

I need a fast car tonight, so I take the keys to one of the Ferraris from the lockbox on the wall beside the elevator.

The sound of the engine drowns out my screaming thoughts for the moment, and I open her up once I get onto the highway.

But the farther I get from Cassie, the worse I feel. Probably because I'm leaving behind the one person I wish was in the passenger seat beside me.

CHAPTER 23

Cassie

I don't cry over boys.

I don't cry over boys.

I repeat the mantra to myself despite the fact that I'm crying because I let a man make me doubt myself.

What Nico texted…

How did he know where I was tonight?

And to just attack me like that?

I don't want to be made to feel like I'm doing something wrong for doing whatever is necessary to keep my brother alive.

Am I glad Nico overstepped his place by gifting me a car and refused to take no for an answer when I said I didn't want it? Yes. But he needs to know I was never going to ask him for money.

Do I want to be dancing for cash? No. But I'm going to do it because I'm good at it and I know I'll be walking out the doors with more money than any 'regular' job I could've gotten.

And how dare he assume I'm getting naked and letting men shove bills in my ass crack.

I haven't gotten naked at all yet, but now I want to just to spite him.

I toss and turn for the rest of the night, only managing to doze off for a few minutes before my alarm wakes me.

Groaning in protest, I drag myself out of bed and get ready. I go with a comfortable outfit of yoga pants and an oversized crewneck sweatshirt. I'm sure as hell not dressing up for them, and I'm not going to show any skin for them to look at or get any ideas with either.

I knock on Sean's door. "Are you ready?"

"Yeah, one second," he calls back, then opens the door. "Are you still sure you want to come?"

"I already ordered our ride. It'll be here in five minutes." I don't bother answering his question. I just turn and head downstairs.

I counted all the cash I made at the clubs, plus what little I could spare from my accounts, and I only have an additional $3,000 to offer on top of the $85,000 I got from selling the Range Rover.

It's a lot, but it's not $100,000.

I know I wouldn't have anything if it wasn't for Nico, but he chose to come at me swinging and be an asshole before I could finish all this, tell him everything, and thank him for his gift.

Now, I'm not doing any of that.

* * * *

The Irish pub we pull up to in Woodlawn Heights reminds me of the place our dad used to take us to back in Boston. He always had to leave us to go and talk to someone after we ordered our food, and didn't come back until Sean and I were almost finished.

Sean's face still holds the markings of the assholes we're about to meet, and I take a deep breath on the sidewalk before stepping inside. I need to be the confident Cassie that takes no shit from anyone so we have a chance of making it out of here in one piece.

I was used to being looked at as an extension of my dad back in the day. Someone to also respect and be spoken to like I was important. So, I pull my shoulders back and walk in there like I know who I am even when I have no idea who I am or where I belong anymore.

Right now, Sean needs me, and I'll pretend to be whomever I need to be if it means we're alive in an hour.

"Sean!" a guy who looks to be just a few years older than me shouts as a greeting, acting like they're two old friends reuniting. He's flanked by two other guys who look like they only speak when ordered to.

189

"Liam," my brother replies, his face neutral.

"Tell me you have something for me," he says, then looks at me with a crooked grin. "Let me guess…you don't have the money and you're here to offer this lovely woman as payment? You must be good if Sean thinks you're worth $100,000."

"She's my sister."

Liam shrugs. "Doesn't answer my question."

"I'm not payment," I sneer, "I *have* the payment."

Laughing, Liam looks to the guys beside him. "Looks like Seany-boy needed his big sister to bail him out. Tell me, sweetheart, where did you get that kind of money?" His eyes travel down my body, which is exactly why I dressed like this.

"I have my ways," I tell him. "But I don't have all of it."

He throws his head back and laughs harder. "That's too bad for your brother then, sweetheart."

"I have $88,000. I can get the rest in a few weeks if you give me time."

"Where is it?" His eyes drift over my empty hands.

"I'll transfer it to you when I have your word you'll give me time for the rest."

"How can I trust you're good for it? Your brother is a degenerate gambler and your father was a conniving bastard who thought he could kill his way to the top and still be respected. And I don't know you at all to trust you. Your family doesn't exactly exude trust."

The air leaves my lungs and I manage to only whisper, "What about my dad?"

Why is he bringing up our dad?

"You didn't know who your dad was, did you? Your brother didn't either," he says smugly.

I look at Sean and he's looking at his feet. "What is he talking about?"

"When I asked my dad about yours, he knew all about him. He said Finn Connelly was an arrogant man who was a trusted captain in the Boston family until he got greedy and decided he wanted to be boss. He took out everyone in his way."

"What are you talking about? He was in FBI custody when the family killed him for turning state's evidence."

All three guys laugh. "No, sweetheart. There was no FBI. Your dad was a ruthless son-of-a-bitch who only had one goal. To be boss."

"No." I shake my head. "You're lying."

"Why would I lie about that? It was ten years ago and in a different city. The lore of your father has been used to teach all of us to watch our backs, even with those who we think we can trust. Which is why I don't trust you, sweetheart."

This whole time I thought my dad was finally going to choose my brother and I. I thought he had enough good left in him to choose his *real* family. I thought he was trying to keep us together.

He lied to me.

Those weren't FBI agents?

He just hired men in suits to trick me and Sean when they were probably just hired muscle to keep him safe from the rest of the family coming after him.

"Why didn't you tell me?" I ask Sean, and he rubs the back of his neck. "How long have you known?"

"They told me after we met."

"And you decided you would use that to try and get an in with us. Isn't that right? As if we'd let the spawn of a man like your father back into the family. His blood runs through your veins."

"Hey," I bark. "Shut the fuck up."

"Ah, she has claws." He smiles. "I like my women with fight in them."

My lip curls in disgust. "Never going to happen."

"Really?" Liam pulls a gun from behind his back and aims it at Sean. "Don't look down on me, sweetheart. Not when I hold the fate of your dear brother."

I grind my teeth together to keep from saying what I really want to. "I'm not sleeping with you."

"I never said anything about sleeping. And it wouldn't be with just me." He winks, and it takes everything in me to hold back from gagging and rolling my eyes.

"You're not touching my sister, Liam," Sean says fiercely. "I'll fucking kill you."

"Big threats from a guy who's still recovering from his last beating."

"Look, here's $3,000 cash." I take the envelope out of my purse and slap it down on the bar. "And if you give me your account information, I'll transfer the other $85,000 that I have."

"Now we're talking. Be right back." Liam disappears into the back of the bar and comes back with an older guy who's wearing a tweed flat cap, a white button down with suspenders, and tan trousers. He reminds me of my grandfather who passed when I was young. He always wore that kind of hat and smoked cigars in his recliner.

"Use this account, little lady," the older gentleman says to me, handing me a slip of paper and a laptop.

I sit at the bar and turn the laptop away from everyone so I can log into my bank account and initiate a transfer.

"There." I log out and clear the browsing data. "You can check your account if you'd like."

The older gentleman does just that and nods. "She's good."

He disappears back behind the bar and I step closer to Sean.

"Alright," Liam says, "you've earned yourself another week to pay the remaining twenty grand."

"Twenty? It's twelve."

He shrugs. "Interest."

I grind my teeth together again to keep my string of curse words and rage from spilling out. "Let's go, Sean."

"Wait a second."

"What?" I ask, annoyed. I just want to leave.

"Just so you remember what's at stake," he says, then waves his fingers forward. His henchmen step forward and grab Sean by his shirt, dragging him away from me.

"Wait! What are you doing?" I shout, and Liam grabs my shoulders to keep me from interfering.

"He's going to stay with us until you bring me the money."

"But—"

"The sooner the better," he interrupts. "I don't like unpaid debts, but I don't like dealing with dead bodies more. Messy business."

"If you kill him, you won't see a dime, and I'll make it my mission to see that you don't live another day either."

He grins like he likes the idea of me trying to hurt him. "That's a pretty big threat."

"It's not a threat. It's a promise." One of the men punches Sean in the stomach and then face as he struggles to break free from their grip, and he instantly slumps in their arms. His ribs are still broken.

"Hey!" I yell, and Liam just laughs.

"He'll be fine as long as you bring me my money."

"Fine!" I shrug him off and push him away from me. "I'll get you the money. Just don't hurt him anymore."

"I can't make any promises. It all depends on how he behaves."

I stare after where they dragged Sean off to, then turn on my heel and leave the bar as quickly as I can.

Once outside, I burn off my suppressed anger by walking for a few blocks.

What am I going to do?

How am I going to get twenty grand before they do something terrible to Sean?

I just...

I want to scream, cry, and throw up, but none of those things are going to help my situation. None of those things are going to get me twenty grand.

I'm alone in this, and it's up to me to save the only family I left.

I'm so desperate, I might have had the courage to tell Nico everything so he could at least give me a hug, if nothing else. I can't do that now, though. Not after what I did to him, and not after what he said to me.

I'm sure he doesn't want anything to do with me now.

I was all in with him yesterday.

I had never felt happier than I did yesterday with him. I let my guard down so he could see I'm falling in love with him, but I fucked it up. In the moment, I thought it was more important to just keep my head down and continue to do what I was doing, not taking his feelings into consideration. At least, not seriously.

I knew he'd be pissed, and I still did it.

I don't deserve him, and I don't deserve his forgiveness. I just hope when this is all over, I'll have the courage to ask for his forgiveness anyway.

CHAPTER 24
Nico

Waking up to a pounding headache is not how I intended to start my day. When I got back to the city, it was still dark and my apartment was too quiet, too cold, and too…empty. I went straight for the whiskey, and didn't stop drinking until I passed out. Which, of course, is what I wanted. I didn't want to have any dreams. I wanted to give my brain a break from all things Cassandra Connelly.

But now that I'm awake, of course she's my first and only thought.

Reaching for my phone, I see I have a text from Rocco.

Rocco: She just left with her brother. Should I follow them?

He texted that a few hours ago, so I call him.

"Hey."

"Did you follow her?" I ask, my voice rough. Jesus, I need some water.

"No, I didn't."

"Why the hell not?"

"I never received a reply and wasn't sure you still wanted me on her after last night."

"Your job isn't to assume anything. I put you on her to protect her. Anywhere she goes from now on, you follow her. Understood?"

"Yes, Sir."

"Is she back yet?"

"Not yet."

"Let me know when she is."

"Will do."

I hang up and rub my eyes. Turning my head, I see my clock and groan. Shit, I slept until the damned afternoon.

I call Stefano next. "Hey, Nico, what's up?"

"I'm back in the city, and I need you to check on something."

"You're back? I thought–"

"We're not talking about this, Stef. I need you to look at Cassie's financials again and tell me if she withdrew all her money yet."

There's only one reason I can think of for them to leave together. With the way he still looks, he'd scare people if he left the house for anything other than a necessity.

"Okay, just give me a few minutes." I wait for him to do his thing, and then he tells me, "Yeah, she transferred it earlier this afternoon."

"Okay," I croak, then clear my throat. She went with her brother to make a payment today. I should've been awake to tell Rocco to follow her. I should've been with her when she went. Her brother clearly can't protect himself. How is he going to protect Cassie? "Can you find out where the McLaughlins operate out of?"

It takes him only a minute to find the answer. "Lucky's Pub in Woodlawn Heights."

"Thanks, Stef."

"Any time, man."

Dragging my ass out of bed, I order food and then take a cold shower to wake myself up. I need to blend in, so I dress casually in black jeans and a black t-shirt.

As I'm lacing up my black boots, I get a notification on my phone that my food was dropped off by security outside my door.

I scarf down the chicken club sandwich and chips, and wash it down with a bottle of water and three aspirin before heading out.

Our building in Manhattan is one we use for everything. The upper three quarters are apartments for the family, and the remaining are offices and conference rooms.

The basement is the same as we have in The Aces, in that there is a whole other world you step into that's not on any city records or accessible by anyone who isn't in the family.

There's a gym, boxing ring, a conference room for our more delicate business conversations to ensure privacy, a fully stocked arsenal of weapons, and a hall of cells to hold anyone when we need to.

Our security is top notch, and to go anywhere in the building, you need your own code, your finger print, and retinal scan. That way we know who is going where at all times, and no one can just walk in and travel from floor to floor.

I make my way down to the garage and choose a more discreet car than the one I came back from AC in.

I drive to the Bronx, and once I get to the Woodlawn Heights neighborhood, my eyes sweep the streets for any sign of Cassie. Lucky's Pub is coming up on the right, and I drive by slowly, but I can't see anything through the windows' tint.

I don't think anyone here will know my face, so I drive around until I find a parking spot and walk back to the pub. Whether she's still here or not, I could use a drink to settle the raging headache I'm still saddled with.

Pushing the door open, my eyes sweep the inside straight away to assess the threat level. Three at the bar, a few couples in the booths, and a table of four guys.

No Cassie or Sean.

I slide up to the bar. "What can I get for you?" the bartender asks.

"Whiskey. Neat."

My eyes continuously scan the bar, and only the eyes of the four guys at the table make their way over to me. I sit and nurse my drink for a few minutes, and then knock back the rest when I get a message from Rocco.

Rocco: She came back alone.

I leave a twenty on the bar and head out.

I close my eyes and lift my face to the sky.

She got out of here alive. She's safe.

I don't know if her brother had a different fate, though, if she returned alone. She sure as hell isn't going to tell me anything after the shit I said to her last night.

I'm such a fucking asshole.

I typed that shit without thinking and pressed send before I knew what I was doing. I let my anger get the better of me, and I wish I could take it all back.

I hate that she lied to me, and I hate that she's still dancing, but that doesn't mean I have the right to degrade her like that.

Whether she wants to admit it or not, she needs me. She needs someone to be on her side when everything she thinks she knows about her life turns out to be a lie.

Me: Let me know if she leaves again. You're going to follow her everywhere.

Rocco: Understood.

I go back to my apartment and pack a bag. A larger one than before. I'm going to stay in Atlantic City as long as it takes. I'm going to be there for her no matter what like I told her I would be. I wasn't ready to be done with her after our weekend together, and I sure as hell am not done with her now.

CHAPTER 25

Cassie

I can't believe what my life has come to. I don't understand how everything got so messed up, so quickly. It's one thing after another that's being thrown at me, and I'm trying to navigate it all, but I'm struggling to find any semblance of control.

I want my life to be how it was.

Before Nico broke my heart. Before he showed up at my job. Before Sean came back from New York. Before I spent the weekend with Nico. Before I asked him to dance. Before I was ruined.

Just...before it all.

But the world doesn't work like that, and I have to keep moving forward if I want to gain control of my life again. The spinning has to stop eventually, and I want to know that I did everything I could to stop it as quickly as possible.

I step into the shower and let the hot water work its magic on my tight muscles. A few tears escape and wash down the drain so I never have to see them for myself. I don't need that. I already saw plenty last night.

Stepping out, I go through the motions of getting ready for another night at Pandemonium. Nico's words aren't going to stop me now. I can't let them, especially when I don't have any other option but to save myself now.

I know I should have been honest with him, but I also never explicitly lied to him. What did he think was going to happen when he got me fired? I'd just give up and think, *oh well?* I tried for one night and that was that?

Now, I'm passed the sad and hurt stages, and have gone straight to angry.

Nico telling me I was only going to dance for him now when he had me on his lap and pressed against his hard cock isn't the same as being in a relationship with someone and them asking me to stop dancing and giving me a good reason to.

I spent one weekend with him, and that's the first thing he has to say to me after a month of nothing?

Is he serious?

If Nico would have talked to me instead of making choices for me, then maybe I would have felt comfortable enough to tell him what's going on and why I'm so desperate for money.

Now, we'll never know, I suppose.

I finally started to let myself see Nico as more. I wanted him to be more.

He's made it clear what he thinks of me, and I doubt he'll ever see me as someone he'll fall in love with now.

Love.

I don't even know what love is.

I thought, just for a moment, I might have been falling in love with Nico. Now I know I was probably just in lust with him and blinded by the sex.

At least, I hope it was just the sex.

It couldn't possibly be the way my heart fluttered every time I was around him. Or the way he was gentle with me when I needed it. Or the way he cared enough about my safety to look into my life when I still had my guard up and wouldn't tell him anything. Or the way I missed him when he wasn't around and loved when he popped up, telling me he needed to see me. And it couldn't possibly be how when he knew he crossed the line, he put all his cards on the table and gave me his entire life to break apart and read.

It couldn't possibly be that I was falling in love with him, the man, at the same time I was desperately falling in love with the way he touched me.

No.

Nope.

It can't be.

Because if that were true, then I'd be screwed.

I can't love someone who doesn't respect me. Although, if I stop and think longer on it, he might respect me too much? That's why he doesn't want me dancing. He said all I had to do was ask him for help and he would have helped.

Did I fuck it all up?

Did I let my stupid pride ruin my chance at something that could've been great?

Great, now I'm passed anger and moving on to regret.

Once again, I don't have time for regrets. Sean needs me, and he's in the hands of the men who already fucked him up once unless I can come up with twenty grand.

I know what I have to do for it.

My path back to Nico will be much harder if I do, but I can't think about that right now. I can only focus on one problem at a time.

My brother's life comes before what I want, how I feel, and my future with Nico.

It has to.

CHAPTER 26

Cassie

I packed my sexiest lingerie I bought on a whim last year when there was a sale to wear on stage tonight. I never wore super sexy outfits to my pole classes, and I haven't had time to go shopping or order anything online, but I know this is going to work just as well with how it's constructed.

I tie the lace cat mask around my head and apply a deep red lipstick to finish off the look.

My eyes stare back at me in the mirror without any emotion despite feeling everything at once. Right now, though, I think defeated is winning out over the rest battling for time in the spotlight.

I had something great for a moment and I ruined it.

I knew I was going to ruin it, too, but I'm just doing what I've done since I was twelve. I'm taking care of my little brother and being the mother figure he was denied.

I take a deep breath and walk confidently to the stage entrance to wait for the emcee to announce my name. A very different practice than at Dark Horse. Pandemonium feels like a movie scene of a stereotypical strip club, whereas Dark Horse felt like a private, dark, sophisticated club you'd only know about through word of mouth.

"And now, welcome to the stage, our newest member of the Pandemonium club, PRETTY KITTY!" he yells, and I cringe on the inside. I didn't come up with that stage name, but when the house mom saw me with the mask, she suggested it and I went with it. It's what Nico called me when he saw me last week, and I thought I'd like having the reminder of him before I took the stage. Now, I don't want the reminder.

With one more deep breath to settle my nerves, I slip into character and saunter out onto stage, blocking out the yells of expletives from the too eager men.

I chose the song "High" by Whethan and Dua Lipa because I did a whole routine to it for my pole dancing class's showcase at the end of last year, so I know exactly when to hit the beats and with which moves.

I practiced so much for that performance, it's second nature to me. So when the second chorus comes and the beat drops, I drop to my knees and untie the bow holding the black lace covering my boobs together. Underneath, I'm still wearing a black leather bra, but it's only the framing of the cups, so my boobs are completely out.

There's an audible cheer, and where I already had money at my feet, more is tossed, in higher denominations this time.

By the time the song is over, it looks like I have more money than I've made in my two nights here combined, splayed out at my feet.

I sashay off the stage, knowing the money will be picked up and delivered to me shortly.

Once I'm through the curtain, I grab the pieces of lace hanging down my back that are still attached to the bra and quickly retie it so I'm covered as my eyes water with the sudden onslaught of emotions I'm experiencing.

Breathe in. Breathe out.

I can do this.

I have to do this.

It's no big deal. It's no big deal. It's no big deal.

Maybe if I repeat it enough to myself, then I'll believe it.

"Cassie," the manager says, startling me out of my meditation.

"Yes?"

"Great job out there."

"Uh, thanks."

"I got another offer for your time. I know you said no yesterday, but tonight's offer is a lot higher."

My gut is telling me to say no, but my brain is telling me to hear him out. "How much?"

"A grand to start."

My eyes bug out. "What?"

"He wanted to make sure you said yes."

"Umm…" I nibble on my bottom lip.

"He's just paying for your time. Anything extra will be extra."

"I'm not having sex with anyone," I tell him straight up, so he knows I have boundaries.

"This isn't a fucking brothel," he says, as if that was offensive for me to insinuate when he's the one telling me extras get me extra money. "We don't pander sex here."

I still want to say no, but I know I'm not going to do any *extras*. This might be the solution I need to get me out of here faster. "I guess I'll do it."

"Great. He'll be in VIP room 3 when you're ready. Don't take too long."

"I won't."

When I get back to the dressing room, the guy in charge of sweeping up the money hands me everything I earned.

"Thanks," I mumble, not making eye contact.

"You're welcome."

I refresh my lipstick and straighten my mask that got slightly askew during my dance.

"You okay?" the girl next to me asks. "I'm Melanie, by the way. Or, Sweet Melody, to everyone out there."

"Hi." I'm able to muster a small smile. "I'm Cassie. And yeah, I think I'm okay. I'm supposed to go to VIP room 3 now, and I'm a little nervous."

"Don't be, honey. It's where the real money is made. They have the money, but you're in charge. Just smile and talk to them like they're the most interesting guy in the world.

Most of the time that's all they want. With a little lap dance on the side." She shrugs.

"Okay." I nod. "Thanks."

"Anytime." Melanie smiles.

I have to walk through the club to get to the VIP area, and men try and stop me, but I just smile and keep walking.

The security guy standing in front of the hallway doesn't even say anything to me. He simply removes the clip of the velvet rope to let me pass and reclips it when I do.

Shoulders back.

Confidence.

It's all a game.

Men are easy.

Take his money and leave.

I repeat those five things in my head until I reach room three.

I don't know if I'm supposed to knock or not, so I knock once to let him know I'm here and then open the door myself.

The man sitting on the purple velvet couch stands when I enter, with a smile spreading across his face. He's actually not bad looking. I wasn't sure what to expect, but it wasn't a good-looking guy who wanted to pay to spend some time with me.

"Pretty Kitty. I can see why they call you that." His eyes run down my body and back up – lingering on my chest before meeting my eyes. "Please, have a seat." He holds his arm out to the couch, and I step around him to sit on the far end of it.

"I can see you're a shy kitty," he teases, his tone like he's talking to a pet rather than a person. "I like that." He sits down next to me. "You weren't shy on stage, though. In fact, I've never been so transfixed before. I knew I needed to talk to you."

"That's sweet, thank you."

"You're welcome." He smirks. "Are you nervous? You seem nervous. We're just talking, Kitty."

I give him a small grin. "I am a little nervous. I'm new to this."

"Your honesty is refreshing. And don't worry, we're just talking. At least, for now." He reaches towards me to move my hair off my shoulder and I freeze, holding completely still, hoping he doesn't touch me. "I love your hair. Is it natural?" His eyes dart down to my lap, and it takes everything in me to not flinch away from him and cross my legs.

This feels like cheating.

I'm not with Nico, and I don't know if I ever was, but this feels like I'm betraying him.

I clear my throat. "It's natural. So, what's your name?" I ask, wanting to get off the subject of my hair and the inevitable, *does the carpet match the drapes?*

He grins. "Brian. But I've been called a few other things before." He winks. "In fact" – he scoots closer to me – "while we're in this room, I insist you call me something else."

I swallow hard, my mouth dry as my body is on high-alert and functioning solely on adrenaline. "What do you want me to call you?" it comes out breathy, which he reads as me trying to be sexy about it when really, I'm just nervous, and he flashes me a predatory grin that sheds all his falsities at once.

He grabs his coat from the couch draped behind him and pulls out a stack of cash. He holds it up between us so I can get a good look, and then tosses it on the table in front of us. "Girls like you always have daddy issues, and that's good for me," he says, touching my hair again.

"Why is that?"

"Because I love spoiling brats like you." He pulls my hair and I gasp, not expecting that. "So when I'm paying for your time, I want you to call me daddy. I want you to tell me how much you love my generosity. I want you to tell me all you're going to do to earn my affection and money."

What the fuck have I gotten myself into?

His eyes take on a different look. They shift away from friendly to something more sinister. His façade completely falling.

"You denied me yesterday, and it seems all it took was more money for you to agree to see me. That tells me all I need to know about you, Pretty Kitty."

"And that is?" I ask, my voice strained. I'm trying to remain calm so I can maneuver myself out of here without getting hurt. Or worse.

"That you're expensive, and not for everyone." He runs his finger down my arm to my hand that's resting on my thigh, where he circles his finger around one of the holes of my fishnets.

"Did I say you could touch me?" I challenge, and he grins, his eyes dancing with mirth. It's time to give him bitch kitty, and not good little kitty.

"Is that the game you want to play?"

"I'm not playing anything. I never said you could touch me."

His eyes dance even more and he reaches into his coat, pulling out another small stack of cash. "How about now? That has to earn me a small touch. Or you can take something off and I won't touch you. I like looking, too." He winks, and my stomach rolls.

I don't want to be here.

I'd rather grovel at Nico's feet and beg him to let me borrow money than be here right now.

What the fuck am I doing?

Fuck my pride, and fuck my stubborn stupidity.

"You don't have enough money to be able to touch me," I tell him. "Or look at me."

I go to stand, and he puts his hand on my thigh, digging his fingers into me to the point of pain.

"Ow, what are you doing?"

"You think you're too good for me? You're a stripper for fuck's sake. You can't be better than me. I pay, and you give me what I want. That's how this works."

"Get your hand off me," I grit out, trying to shove him away from me. He doesn't budge, and instead pins me down by wrapping his other hand around my bicep. "Get off me!" I say louder, but he just smiles.

"I like some fight in a woman. That's what makes the chase all the more fun." He tries to kiss me, so I turn my face away so all he gets is my cheek. "But not too much fight," he adds.

He drags me away from the corner of the couch and goes to straddle me to pin me down where I know it'll be harder to escape.

That's when the reality of what's about to happen hits me and I freeze for a split second before kicking it into high gear and fighting like hell any way I can.

He may have a hold of my leg and arm, but I'm still able to reach between his legs to grab his dick. I squeeze him as hard as I can and he yelps out a squeal that I find immensely satisfying.

But the next thing I know, the back of his hand is connecting with my cheek, and my fears turn to pure anger.

I'm angry I put myself in this situation. I knew coming in this room was a bad idea from the start.

I'm angry this piece of shit thinks he can touch me because he tossed some money on the table.

I'm angry I pushed Nico away again, when all I want to do is pull him closer.

I wish he was here.

I want to tell him how sorry I am and that I'll do anything to gain his trust back and promise to never lie to him again.

I want to be able to face him again and still be only his. I don't want this guy's hands on me, in me, or anywhere near me.

I twist his dick, and when his grip on my thigh loosens, I knee him in the dick and claw at his face – raking my nails down his cheek and neck.

Brian lets out a scream and covers his face, which gives me the opportunity to push him away and get out from under him.

I make a beeline for the door and yank it open. These stupid heels are slowing me down, but it doesn't matter because I hear the angry voice of an angel and run straight towards it.

I hit a wall of muscle and feel arms wrap around me that let me know I'm safe. "Help me. Please." My voice is raw, and it comes out as a broken plea while tears stream down my face.

"I've got you, Cassandra," Nico assures me, and I'm calm for only a moment before he holds me at arm's length to look me over. I cower away from his gaze and wrap my arms around my middle. "What happened?"

"He...I didn't want him to touch me."

Nico doesn't say a word. I can't look him in the eyes because I don't want to see the disappointment or regret in them.

I don't know what he's seeing right now, but I watch as his hands turn to fists and he storms past me and right into the room I just ran out of.

CHAPTER 27
Nico

My vision tunnels.

No one fucking touches my girl.

Cassie's crying and shaking, and holding herself like she wishes she had on ten layers of clothes.

My hands fist at my sides and I storm past her into the room she just ran out of. The asshole she was with is sitting on the couch dabbing his face with a napkin. I see Cassie got him pretty good. Good. But I'm going to do much worse.

"Who the fuck are you?" he asks, wincing and cupping his dick.

"I'm here to finish what she started."

"What?"

My legs eat up the rest of the distance between us in a fraction of a second, and my fist is connecting with his face before he has time to block me.

I don't stop there, either.

I hit him again and again until his face is bloody and unrecognizable. Good. Now he's even uglier.

Cassie asked for my help. She finally asked for my help and I'm not going to let her down.

He grunts and groans every time my fist connects with him, and it isn't until a gentle hand wraps around my arm that's fisting his shirt that I hold back my next strike.

"Nico," Cassie says in a soothing voice. "Stop before you kill him."

"He deserves it," I tell her harshly, my chest heaving with every breath. Tears are streaming down her face and her pretty blue eyes are wide and pleading with me to listen to her. All I hear is the kill him part, though.

"I don't want that. It's my fault."

"It's not," I growl, and hit him twice more before his head starts to loll to the side and Cassie's grip on my arm tightens.

"Nico!" she yells. "Stop! Please!"

"Did he touch you?" I manage to ask through my haze of anger.

"No, I didn't let him. He grabbed my arm and leg, but nothing more. I don't want you to kill him for me."

"You're crying. That's the only reason I need to kill him."

"Nico, please. I just want you to take me home. Leave him here for someone else to deal with."

Her hand starts to rub up and down my forearm, goading me to loosen my grip on his shirt.

"Please," she repeats. "Take me home."

Her eyes are still pleading with me, and I can't deny her when she's looking at me like that.

My hand that's gripping his shirt opens, and she slips hers in its place.

We walk only a few steps before she stumbles in her shoes. She sniffs and swipes away a few more tears as she looks down at her feet. "I really want to take these off."

"I've got you, baby." I sweep her up into my arms and cradle her to my chest.

I expect her to tell me no, or that she can walk herself, but she just snuggles closer to me and wraps her arms around my neck.

I walk her out of there, and those who dare look our way, quickly divert their gaze when I meet theirs.

Rocco opens the passenger door of my car for me and I gently deposit her onto the seat. I close the door and tell him, "Go in there and get her things from the dressing room."

"Got it." He nods and heads inside.

Pulling out my phone, I call Alec. "Hey, what's up?"

"I want Pandemonium burned to the fucking ground," I growl out, still needing to burn my anger off.

"Okay," he agrees without hesitation.

"There's a guy in there with a fucked-up face who may cry lawsuit or whatever bullshit he'll come up with for me rearranging his face. I don't give a fuck. Can you have it taken care of if he's brought to the hospital?"

"Of course. Should I bother asking why we're burning it down?"

"Because I don't want any part of it standing by the morning. After what happened to Cassie tonight…" I look back at the car where she's waiting for me. "Don't fucking ask for details. If I ever have to look at that building again, I'm going to burn it down myself, and it won't be carefully."

"I'll have Dante come down and take care of it. He'll find a reason to get everyone out and then take care of it carefully and quietly."

"Good." I hang up, and Rocco comes back with Cassie's things just in time.

I fold myself into the car and drive off to Cassie's house with neither of us saying a word. I'm still too wound up to trust anything that comes out of my mouth, and Cassie is curled up close to the door – as far away from me as she can get. She's shaking from the adrenalin wearing off, and rips the mask off her face, tossing it into the back seat.

I park in her driveway and get out straight away. I grab her bag from the back seat and take her keys from the side pocket and put them in mine. I take my jacket off as I round the car and hold it out for her when I open her door.

"Put this on," I tell her, and she shoves her arms in immediately.

She wraps it around her chest to cover herself, but when she looks down at her legs, I see more tears stream down her face. "I've got you, baby," I tell her again, and lift her up into my arms where she belongs.

Carrying her to the door, I maneuver her with one hand to get her keys out of my pocket and unlock it. I carry her right upstairs and into the bathroom, sitting her down on the closed toilet seat.

"I can give you a minute to undress yourself if you'd prefer, but I'd rather help you."

She shakes her head no. "Stay."

Thank God, because she was going to have to push me out the door to get me to leave.

I kneel down on one leg and lift her feet one at a time to remove her heels. I don't even know how she can walk in these things.

I turn on the water of the shower so it can warm up while I take my jacket off her. When I go for the lingerie she has on, she wraps her arms over her stomach.

"Don't do that, Cassie. Just let me help you so you can wash him off you, okay? Don't shy away from me like you don't want me to see you."

"It's not that," she whispers, her voice hoarse. "I'm ashamed."

I take her face in my hands and swipe her tears away. "Never be ashamed in front of me. I'll take care of you."

She gives me a small nod, and I continue to undress her. Under any other circumstances, I would find her outfit the sexiest thing I'd ever seen, but not right now. Now, all I see is the raw Cassandra she keeps hidden under the layers of sass, stubbornness, and fear. All to protect herself from the world and whoever wants to get close to her, to ensure they never do.

Her veil is down right now. I see the young and vulnerable Cassandra she hasn't let herself be for quite some time.

Once she's fully undressed, I quickly shed my clothes and guide her into the shower. I wash her carefully, and my anger spikes when she winces as my hand glides over a part of her arm and thigh where I see marks forming.

That fucking bastard deserved more than he got for hurting her.

Turning her around, I methodically shampoo and condition her hair, and massage her scalp as I rinse her off. Cassie hums her approval, and her eyes remain closed while I turn her back to face me and the water cascades over her.

I wash myself next, then trade places with her to rinse off, and her eyes remain cast downward as I pat the both of us dry.

She won't look me in the eyes.

I need to see hers, but I know she needs a little time to gather herself.

I wrap a towel around her and reach for another on the shelf when Cassie gasps. My heartrate spikes. "What? What's wrong?" I ask frantically.

"Your hand," she says, taking my right hand in hers. She holds it gently in her outstretched palm. "Go sit on my bed and wait for me. I'll fix you up."

I won't turn down her undivided attention, so I do as she says, and find her room down the hall. I sit on the end of her bed and look around. Her room is made up of neutral colors. It's quite different than how I see her. She's vibrant and full of spice and life, so I can only assume this is her safe space. A calm place where she can retreat to and none of the outside noise she deals with crosses over that threshold.

Cassie hurries into her room with her arms full of first aid supplies and a worried look marring her beautiful face. She drops to her knees in front of me and dumps the supplies on the floor. She takes my hand in hers again and starts to dab a cotton ball soaked in hydrogen peroxide over my cuts.

I hadn't realized how torn up my knuckles were before this moment, because frankly, I didn't, and still don't, care. But now I can see how I ripped my knuckles open on that prick's face. I don't even feel it yet, but Cassie thinks I do, because her brows are pinched together in deep concentration and she's biting her perfect puffy lower lip as she dabs carefully so she doesn't hurt me.

She blows cool air over my knuckles, and I feel the breeze blowing off the last cobwebs around my heart. She's fucking got me. She's taking up all the space in me she can, and I never want her to leave.

Cassie stays focused while she dabs on antibacterial cream with a cotton swab, and then gently covers the wounds with a large piece of gauze before wrapping my hand in bandage tape to keep it in place.

I would tell her it's not necessary, but I like her fussing over me.

When she finally looks up at me, I'm punched in the gut with how crushed she looks. "Thank you for saving me. You got there at just the right moment." She launches herself into my arms and I hold her tight. "I'm sorry. I'm so sorry for everything," she says in my ear. "I shouldn't have left you, I shouldn't have lied, and I shouldn't have kept you in the dark about everything that's going on with me. I don't want to lie to you ever again, and I promise I won't."

"*Piccante*," I croon. I stand and she locks her legs around as I carry her around the bed to lay us down. "*Piccante*." I push her wet strands of hair over her shoulder and cup her cheek. "I'm sorry for what I said to you. You didn't deserve that."

"I did. I messed up. I messed everything up." Her throat works around a swallow. "I thought I had to do everything on my own because he's my brother, which meant he was my problem, and mine alone. But I guess it took what happened tonight to realize how stupid I was being. I was begging for you in my head, Nico. And then you appeared." The corners of her lips lift just the slightest. "Why did you come for me when you knew I was there?"

"I wasn't going to let you go so easily. I think we both assumed some things about the other and it stood in our way. I assumed getting you fired would be the end of it, and when it wasn't, I was mad at myself, not you. I should've known. I should've made you accept my help."

"Nico," she says softly, in a calming voice that sits well in my soul. "It's cute that you think you can make me do anything."

The small chuckle that leaves me takes me by surprise and her small smile widens. "Yes, that's true."

"But I shouldn't have been so stubborn. I'm going to work on that."

"Does that mean you'll finally let me help you? Because money means nothing to me. There's always more money to be made, but there's only one you. And I need you, Cassie."

"You do?" The spark of hope in her voice is endearing.

"Yes, Cassandra. I do."

"I need you, too," she tells me, brushing her fingertips across my cheek. "I need you more than you know. More than I've said or shown you. I've thought about you every day since I left you after our weekend together. I actually dreamt of you coming to me. That you would just show up and kiss me and tell me you just had to have me," she says wistfully, laughing to herself like it was a silly thing to say.

I rub my thumb against her cheek. "I should've done that."

"Everything happens for a reason. Our story was meant to be written this way."

"Two puzzle pieces finally finding the perfect fit?"

She gives me one of her sweet smiles that makes my heart fucking grow with how much I love seeing it. I want to make sure I give her a reason to keep smiling like that.

"Yes. Exactly," she whispers, and her eyes water again.

"Please don't cry, *piccante*."

"It's because you're being sweet and I'm happy." She caresses my cheek. "Don't worry."

"I'll always worry about you. I want to make you happy, not sad. I don't want to cause you pain."

"We don't know the future, Nico. Maybe you or I will do something stupid one day, thinking we're helping the other or trying not to worry them. The only way we can combat that is with honesty. I promise to be honest with you, even when it's hard."

"I appreciate that. I promise to always be honest with you, too. Which is a good segway in telling you that after I found out your brother was in trouble with the McLaughlin family, I've had someone watching over your house every night to make sure no one came to harm either of you while you were the most vulnerable."

"That's really sweet," she says, surprising me.

"It is?"

"Yes." She laughs, then sobers quickly. "Is that how you knew I was dancing again?"

"It is." I nod. "It's also how I knew you were there again tonight."

"Since you saved me, I'm glad you had me followed. Are you still going to have me followed now?"

"Not if you're with me all the time to keep you safe myself."

"Okay."

"Okay?"

"Yes, I'm more than okay with that," she says, leaning forward to plant a kiss on my cheek. "I'm scared for my brother, Nico."

"What happened today? You made the drop with the money at Lucky's Pub, but you came back alone."

"I gave them the $3,000 in cash I had and then wired them the $85,000 I got for the car you gave me." Her eyes shift away and I urge her back to look at me with a little nudge of her jaw.

"Hey, it's okay. You know I did it on purpose, right?"

"Yes, I know. I figured it out when you didn't ask me why it wasn't in the driveway."

"I was surprised you didn't march right over to me to either hand me the keys or the money you got for it just to spite me."

"I knew you'd refuse the keys, and I chose to accept the gift, telling myself the argument wasn't worth it."

"You're so fucking cute." I give her a quick kiss on the lips and her cheeks turn pink with a pretty blush. "Keep going. What happened when you were there?"

"They told me my dad wasn't who I thought he was. My dad wasn't a nice guy, but I never thought he was a *bad* guy. He told me he was going to turn state's evidence on the family because they framed him for some stuff. He said the three of us would go into witness protection and move out west to start over.

"He lied to me, Nico. He was killing his way to the top. And the supposed FBI agents we were with at the motel when he was killed were just hired muscle to protect him while he did whatever he was doing. I mean, how was he going to explain his lies to me if his plan worked and we were still in Boston and he was boss?" I can see the panic in her eyes taking over. "Was he going to get rid of Sean and I? Did he even want us? Was he going to ship us off somewhere and pretend he'd meet us later and then never show? Or worse?"

"Shh, baby." I rub her back until she relaxes again. "I'm so sorry, Cassie."

"And Sean knew. He found out last year when he met those guys and he never told me."

"How does one bring that kind of thing up?"

"I know. But still… Everything I know and remember about my dad is a lie. I thought he wanted to keep his family together and was doing what he could to make that happen. I thought he loved us."

"He did, Cassie," I assure her. "He just fell into the trap of greed and power the life we live puts so tauntingly in front of us. It can make even the strongest succumb to it more often than not."

"Does that mean you'll fall into that trap? Or someone else in your family? How do you know when someone is genuine or not?"

"There are men who work for us that have tried to be greedy, but we shut them down when we find out. And we always find out. They don't pose much of a threat because only the immediate family holds the power positions, and we all know our roles in the family and businesses. We've been through some tough shit together since we were kids and we respect each other too much to think one is better than the other. We get paid the same, too, so there's no greed to chase."

"Okay."

"I told you we're not the same as the McLaughlins, or even any of the other three families?"

"Three?"

"Yes. There were five, including us, until recently. Now, there's only four."

"Did you have something to do with that?" she asks bravely.

"Yes," I tell her honestly. "They deserved to be wiped out. They were behind my father and uncle's deaths, and ruined Angela's life. She's with my cousin, Luca. Her story isn't mine to share, though."

"Oh," Cassie says softly. "Then they deserved it," she concludes.

"Trust me, they did."

"I trust you."

"Do you trust me to help you out of the situation you're in?"

"Yes." Her eyes water again. "Sean owed $85,000 originally. I sold my car and he gave them $5,000. Then when he got beaten up, he told me they wanted an extra $20,000 for the inconvenience of having to find him because they thought he fled. So, I had to find a way to come up with $100,000. Because you insisted on tricking me, I was lucky enough to have $88,000 to give them. Now, they're keeping him until I can pay another twenty. Interest again, of course.

"That's why I had to find another job, and that's why I agreed to go to that room tonight. I didn't want to last night when I was first asked, and I didn't want to tonight either. But I thought I had no other choice, and that stupid manager said all I had to do was talk to the guy. I didn't have to do anything I didn't want. But it escaladed pretty quickly and I…"

Cassie's breathing comes quicker and I pull her closer. "I've got you now."

She takes in a deep, shaky breath. "I know."

"And I'll get your brother back for you. I don't want you to worry about it anymore." I rub small circles up and down her back, and she relaxes further under my touch.

"Only if you let me pay you back somehow."

"You can pay me back by being mine. You're all I need."

"Nico," she says softly, raking her fingers through my wet hair. "No one's chosen me like you before. I've never been first."

"Get used to being first, *piccante*." I tilt her chin up and give her a slow kiss that grows into more pretty damn quickly when she pushes me onto my back and straddles me.

Her hips rock against me, and with the only thing separating us being our towels, I rip hers away from her body and roll us back over so I can pull mine free and line myself right up to her waiting pussy.

I thrust inside her, all the way to the hilt in one motion, and her mouth tears away from mine to let out a moan that has my dick so hard, I could pound nails into wood.

I fuck her hard so I can hear that throaty moan again.

I fuck her hard so she knows she's mine.

I want her to know this is how it'll be for the rest of her life.

Her orgasm comes on fast and without warning, and her pussy seizes around me, flooding my cock with her come.

I fuck her through it, and the wet sound of us slapping together is driving me fucking wild and drives me to fuck her even harder.

Cassie gasps and moans, and claws at my shoulders while her body builds to another orgasm.

"Get used to being first forever," I tell her, and her wild eyes meet mine as she comes apart for a second time.

The pure fucking bliss on her face is because of me, and I pump into her twice more before I'm right there with her, spilling my come into her and staking my claim. No other man has done that, and no other will ever again.

CHAPTER 28

Cassie

Nico keeps his arms firmly around me the rest of the night, and I wake up having had the best night's sleep of my life.

Everything is out in the open.

No secrets. No more lying.

"You awake, *piccante*?"

"Mmhmm," I hum, turning my face towards him and planting a little kiss to his chest. "Can you order me coffee?"

He shakes with a short laugh. "Yeah, I can do that. You stay here and I'll come and get you when it's here."

"Okay." He won't get an argument from me. This bed is comfortable.

When Nico stands, I get a nice view of his perfect ass, along with the ocean beyond the wall of windows.

I could get used to this. I wonder what the view from his place in New York looks like.

I stare out at the ocean for a while, and then slide out of bed to use the bathroom. I put on one of the white robes hanging behind the door and find Nico sitting at the round dining table off the kitchen, reading the newspaper with the local news on the TV with the volume down.

My eyes skirt over the screen at first, but go back when I see the name Pandemonium on the bottom.

What the…?

Footage of the club on fire comes onto the screen and I gasp. "Nico, what did you do?"

"Huh?" he says casually, looking up from the newspaper to see where I'm looking. "Oh, that. It was necessary."

"Was it?"

"Yes. I can't know that place is still standing or I'll going fucking crazy."

"I think you already have judging by the fact you had it burned down."

"It was a decision made in anger, but one I'm still glad I made. I don't want anyone who saw you dance be able to go back there and remember you. I don't want that piece of shit from last night to be able to go back there and do that to someone else. Not that he'll be able to do much with the way I left him. I didn't want them in business anymore, and now they're not."

That's the most insane thing I've ever heard. Crazy, insane, and completely unnecessary. But I love that he did it all the same. So, I guess I'm a little crazy too.

"Are you mad?" he asks, looking over his shoulder at me, still frozen by the doorway.

I shake my head. "No."

"Good. Come sit. Breakfast will be here in a few minutes."

"You're crazy," I whisper, shaking my head.

He gives me one of his smiles that leaves me stunned by how handsome he is. "It seems I'm only crazy when it involves you."

"Let's keep it that way." I place my hand on his shoulder and kiss his cheek before taking the seat beside him that faces the windows.

When the food arrives, I eagerly wait for Nico to place the coffee carafe on the table and then pour myself a steaming cup of happiness. I add a little cream to it and bring it to my nose to inhale the hazelnut scent. By the time I take a sip, I realize Nico is looking at me like I'm doing something fascinating.

"Yes?"

"Nothing. I'm just realizing one of my fantasies is playing out before my eyes."

Oh...

I smile behind my cup, remembering what he said about waking up with him and having breakfast in my robe and letting it slip open.

I sip my coffee and take a piece of bacon off my plate. Biting into it, I place my coffee down and covertly untie the belt on the robe.

Reaching to the middle of the table for the salt and pepper, I sprinkle a little of each on my eggs and let my robe fall open when I place them back.

I angle myself towards Nico and put on a little show crossing my legs so he can see his fantasy as a reality.

"Fuck, baby," he groans, scraping his teeth over his lower lip.

"Hmm?" I casually go about buttering my pancakes and pouring syrup over them while he sits back and drinks his coffee, keeping his eyes on me. "Your food's getting cold," I tell him.

"It'll be fine."

"Whatever you say."

"It is." He smirks.

I'll let him have his fill. He came to my rescue last night. But when a drop of syrup drips from my fork onto my chest, he groans and snaps. Grabbing the seat of my chair, he pulls me towards him and bands his arm around my back while his mouth descends on my chest.

His hot tongue swipes up the syrup. "Delicious."

"It's even better on the food. You should eat."

"It's better on you, *piccante*. Trust me."

"I'll have to. I can't lick it off my own chest."

"I'd be hot if you could."

Laughing, I go about eating and drinking the best coffee I've ever had, blissfully content.

That is, until it hits me that my brother is being held hostage by a family who hates mine.

I place my fork down and wrap my robe around me again. "Nico, as much as I'd like to think everything is perfect right now – which it almost is – my brother needs me. I don't know what they're doing to him."

"Hey," Nico says gently, squeezing my thigh. "You said you trusted me to take care of it, and I am."

"How?"

"I called Leo and told him what's going on. He's arranging the money now and we'll meet him in New York this afternoon to get your brother back."

"Really?" I ask, surprised and elated.

"Yes."

"Thank you!" I launch myself at him and he holds me tight. "I promise to pay you back very thoroughly afterwards," I whisper in his ear, and his arms tighten around me.

"I'd never turn down an offer like that, *la mia rossa piccante.*"

CHAPTER 29

Cassie

When we arrive at the Carfano building in Manhattan, Nico takes me up to one of their conference rooms, and I get a firsthand look at how tight their security is.

"This seems like a safe building," I say casually.

"It is," Nico confirms. "We take safety seriously. You'll get used to it."

I smile up at him. "Is that so?"

"Yes, because you're going to be living here soon, and it'll become second nature to go through the motions of the code, fingerprint, and eye scan."

My head jerks back, surprised. "I'll be living here with you soon?"

"You'll graduate first, of course. But then yes, you'll be living with me."

"Did you not think to ask me?"

Nico pulls me into an empty office before we reach the conference room and backs me up against the nearest wall, caging me in with his strong arms on either side of my head.

"Will you please move to New York and live with me, *la mia rossa piccante*? You can do anything you want with my apartment to make it a home you love. It's a little cold right now, but I know you'll warm it right up just by being there."

I lift my chin defiantly. "What else do I get if I agree?"

He smirks, turning on the charm and making my legs feel like they won't support me for long. "You get to have whatever you want, whenever you want it."

"Whatever I want, whenever I want it?"

"Yes." He runs his nose down the bridge of mine and my breath hitches. He knows he already has me. "You can have everything your heart desires and then some."

"My heart desires just one thing. One thing I need and can't live without. Anything else will just be a bonus."

He steps closer to me so his body is a mere inch away. Enough for me to feel his body like a magnet fighting its pair. "And what is it your heart desires, Cassandra?" He presses his forehead to mine and his lips hover just above mine.

"You. My heart desires just you. You in all sorts of dirty ways." I smile. "But also in the gentle way you treat me when I need it. The dominance you use when I don't want to be in control anymore. And especially in the way you accept me wholeheartedly."

"I do, baby. Even when you're sassy and stubborn, and yelling at me. I want all of you. I love all of you."

"What?" My breath just left my body.

"You heard me, Cassandra. I don't know how else this feeling can be described. The addiction I've had since I first laid eyes on you. The way I didn't want to let you go even after spending every minute of those three days with you, when I'd usually be bored after the first night with a woman.

"The way your eyes shine when they look at me. It's like I'm looking into the ocean on a bright summer morning. The way your hair lights my bed on fire as much as our bodies do. The way you were on my mind every day and night since the moment I met you, and my need for you never diminished. It's only gotten stronger every time I'm around you, too. The way I want to be with you – *all the time*," he emphasizes, and I don't know how much more my heart can take before I pass out or have a heart attack.

"We'd be here all day if I listed every little thing, but I have more. Trust me. I discovered a new one today. The way you go about taking your first sip of coffee in the morning. I can't wait to watch you drink a cup every morning."

I can't take any more.

I grab his suit jacket lapels and close the distance between us, fusing my lips to his in a kiss that I pour every single ounce of the built-up emotions he just caused in me into.

Every ounce of love.

I can't get close enough to him.

I press my chest to his and have the urge to climb him like a fucking tree to get even closer.

Nico breaks the kiss first, and I grunt my disapproval, which has him smiling against my lips. "*Piccante*, we have to slow down or I'll be fucking you against the wall with my family waiting for us a few rooms down."

"I love you, too, Nico," I blurt out, and for a second, I think he stops breathing.

"Say it again," he growls, pulling back to look into my eyes.

"I love you, Nico." I barely finish getting his name out before his lips are back on mine, even more intensely now. His tongue delves into my mouth and tangles with mine in the hottest, messiest kiss of my life that has my body igniting and my panties flooding.

Nico pulls away again, and I grunt my protest a second time. His ragged breathing makes me feel a thousand feet tall, in that I can make this man weak for me.

"I didn't expect you to say it back," he admits. "I didn't need you to say it back. I just needed to tell you, and I would've loved you hard enough for the both of us until you were ready to tell me."

I didn't think my heart could take any more, and then Nico goes and says that. It's going to explode in my chest if he's not careful.

I reach up and wrap my arms around him, burying my face in his neck. I kiss his exposed skin above the collar of his shirt and murmur against him, "I hate that you think I wouldn't say it. That I don't feel it."

"No, baby." He brings my face back in front of him. "I know how you feel. I see it in your eyes. I just thought you'd need more time to let *yourself* feel it and know it's true enough to tell me."

"You're too kind and understanding to be real. How do you know me so well when it hasn't even been that long?"

He gives me one of his sexy smiles. "I don't know. I fucking love it, though."

"I guess that just proves you're my missing piece."

"Fuck yeah, I am, *piccante.*" Nico kisses me hard and fast, and then steps back, leaving me off kilter. "We shouldn't keep my family waiting any longer." He smirks, and my cheeks heat.

"You made me forget why we were here." I quickly run my fingers through my hair and swipe at my lips and under my eyes to make sure my makeup is still in place.

"You look perfect." He takes my hand. "Let's go."

Walking into the conference room hand-in-hand with Nico while all eyes are on us feels empowering. Like I'm on stage again.

And holy Jesus, this family has good genes. Every man at the table has the air of power and dominance, with faces that could bring any woman they want to their knees.

I should know. Nico has had me ready to drop to my knees from the start.

"Cassie, meet Leo, Luca, Stefano, Marco, and Gabriel." He points to each of them around the table. "Guys, this is Cassandra Connelly. She's mine." I look up to see his little boy grin, and shake my head, rolling my eyes.

"Hi, everyone," I greet with a little wave. "Thank you for helping me and my brother. I know we're not your problem, and I appreciate it."

"We always help family," Leo says, and the others nod their agreement.

"I'm not family," I say, and Nico squeezes my hand.

"What did we just talk about not five minutes ago, *piccante*?" he asks quietly. "You're family now."

"Okay," I say shyly, my eyes going from his to the floor so everyone in the room doesn't see how crazy I am for Nico, and how much I want him to take me up to his apartment and fuck me senseless.

"The money is ready to go," Marco says, pushing a duffel bag across the table towards us.

"And I'll monitor you from here," Stefano tells us. He's the one Nico wrote in his note compiled the packet for me. Which means he's also the one who dug into my life for Nico.

The resident tech guy, I assume.

I don't shy away from him, and instead look him dead in the eyes so he's the one who's uncomfortable and looks away, clearing his throat.

"You'll kill him with those eyes, Cassie," Nico says, nudging my shoulder playfully. "Give him a break. He was doing his job."

"You carry a lot of secrets, don't you?" I ask him.

"I do," Stefano confirms. "And they stay with me."

His eyes are unwavering with his words, making me feel his sincerity. "Thank you." I nod, and he gives me one of his own, appreciating my understanding of his burden.

"I'll drive you two and remain in the car at the curb," Gabriel tells me.

"And I'll be driving Leo," Marco adds.

"Are you sure we need so many people?" I ask to no one in particular, but glance up at Nico.

"We're making a united front so they know who they're dealing with and won't keep asking you for more money or get your brother back into debt."

"I don't know how to keep him out of trouble after this. He already almost gambled the other night, but I was able to convince him to come home before he did."

"I've thought of that," Leo continues. "He needs to get away from here and what he's used to. I can send him to Miami and he'll help our cousins, Saverio and Matteo, run our club down there."

"Miami?" I balk, surprised by the offer. "Is that any better than here to keep him from gambling?"

"We'll give him a purpose. Responsibility. Plus, the sun and women down there will motivate him to stay in line."

I don't want to agree for him, but I think a change of scenery would do Sean well. "We can give him the choice, but it'll have to be his choice. Thank you for the offer. I wasn't expecting that."

"We'll help you and your brother any way you need."

"Thank you."

Nico squeezes my hand and I squeeze his back to let him know how much I appreciate him. I didn't expect his family to be like this. They're all ready and willing to band together to help me and Sean when they don't know us. I know I'm with Nico, and I know he said family comes first, but to see it, hear it, and experience it firsthand is heartwarming. Like real families still exist.

"I don't know where they're keeping him. We met at Lucky's Pub yesterday and they dragged him down the back hall, but I don't know if he's still there."

"We do. I hacked into their security cameras in and around the pub, and he never left."

"Oh, okay. Good then. At least we know where he is."

"He'll be fine, *piccante*. It's only been a day," Nico reminds me.

"Then let's go."

"You should stay here with Stef and Luca," Leo suggests, and my head whips back towards him.

"That's not going to happen. I already met that asshole yesterday and he doesn't scare me. He's expecting me, and that's who he's going to get. You can come if you want as backup, but I need to be there."

"Be your backup?" Leo swipes his hand over his mouth to try and hide his smile, but I catch it.

"I like her," Marco says, giving Nico a nod of approval, which has him rumbling next to me.

"I see why you call her *piccante*," Gabriel adds, throwing me a wink.

"That's enough," Nico growls, and the men at the table smirk. They like seeing him mad over me, and I won't lie, I like it too. It's sweet. In a possessive, alpha way that makes me want to jump him again. "Let's go."

Nico grabs the duffel of money and we all head down to the garage. This time, we get into a blacked-out Range Rover that seems like it's fitted with enough extras to withstand a firefight.

Our SUV leads the way to Woodlawn Heights with Leo's following.

"Why aren't we doing this ourselves?" I ask Nico. "Do you think we need so many extra people? What if it leads to conflict?"

"I won't let anything happen to you, Cassie. I promise."

"I know. I just… It was a lot for me to accept the help to begin with. Now, most of your family is involved, and…" I shake my head.

"Hey," he says, turning my face towards his. "This is what we do. We plan and execute. Together. You're not in this alone anymore. You don't *need* to be in this alone anymore."

I relax only the slightest, still chewing on my bottom lip as we make our way to the Bronx. When we reach the pub, Gabriel pulls up to the open spot, one car down from the front doors, and the other SUV double parks beside us.

We get out, and I take the lead, not even waiting for Nico or Leo. I walk right into the bar and scan the inside for that piece of shit, Liam. He's sitting at a table towards the back with his two goons.

"Where's my brother?" I demand, and Liam looks up with that stupid shit-eating-grin he wore yesterday.

"Back so soon, sweetheart? I assume you have my money then? And if not, it's still good to see such a fiery, beautiful woman two days in a row. Especially if you're here to offer me an alternate form of payment."

"Watch your fucking mouth," Nico snarls from right behind me.

"Ah, so you're taken. Damn it." Standing, he and his henchmen walk up to us.

"I am," I confirm. "Not that you ever had a chance. Where's Sean? I have your money."

"Already? How did you get it so fast?" he asks, giving me another crooked grin and a wink.

"If you don't watch how you speak to her, you won't get your money or be breathing in the next five minutes."

I ignore Nico's threats and step towards Liam, which results in a grunt of disapproval from him. I know exactly how to play this idiot. "Actually, I got it exactly how you think," I tell Liam, smirking. "I'm as good as you're thinking." It's my turn to throw him a wink, and he laughs. "Now, bring my brother out or my man will follow through on his threats."

Liam laughs and takes a step back. "Go get him," he tells the guy on his right.

"I should've asked for more money if I knew you had such a generous benefactor."

I know right away Nico isn't going to take one more insult out of this guy's mouth.

"Now you don't get any money," Nico says calmly. Too calmly. And Liam just laughs. I think he has a few screws loose for taunting Nico and not realizing the danger he's in or who he's talking to.

"Is that right? And who are you to threaten me and get away with it?"

"Nico Carfano."

Liam's eyes flash with recognition, and his smile is wiped from his stupid face.

Leo takes a step forward to stand right beside me. "And Leo Carfano. It's nice to meet you, Liam. Every encounter I've had with the McLaughlin family has always been somewhat cordial. Until now."

Liam doesn't say anything, but it looks like he's going to shit a brick.

"So," Leo continues, "we're going to call the rest of this debt cleared since you caused us the trouble of coming all the way here. You won't come after Sean or Cassie or anyone associated with them from this moment forward. If we continue to have an issue, then I'll be forced to tell Conor how you conducted business with my family."

"Yes, Mr. Carfano. I understand," he says eagerly.

Wow, are you serious?

Leo has rendered this idiot speechless and turned him into a complacent soldier with manners in seconds. He must have a big reputation and hold a lot of power in this city if his name and presence hold such weight that it crosses over to the Irish mob as if he was their boss barking out orders.

I look past Liam and see Sean being led towards us. Luckily, he doesn't look any worse than yesterday besides dark circles under his eyes like he didn't get any sleep.

"Sean!" I breathe a sigh of relief and push past Liam to give him a hug.

"Hey, Cass. You're early," he jokes, coughing on a short laugh.

"I'm just glad I'm not too late. How are you?"

"Fine. I'm ready to get out of here."

"Let's go." I loop my arm through Sean's and lead him out, with Nico and Leo following close behind.

"Sean, you'll ride with me. I have something to discuss with you," Leo says, his tone leaving no room for discussion, but Sean still looks at me.

"Listen to what he has to say, Sean," I tell him, and give him a hug.

"I will. Thank you for saving my ass. I promise I'll be better."

"I believe in you." I kiss his cheek and he gets in the SUV with Leo while Nico opens the back door for me and I climb up inside.

"He'll be fine, Cassie," Nico consoles, and I lean my head on his shoulder.

"I know. I hope he takes Leo up on his offer. It was really nice of him."

"He has his moments."

"I like that Liam was scared of him." I smile. "That guy needs to be punched in the face."

"I would've gladly done it, but you had him under your thumb."

"It's easy to play someone so simple with a one-track mind."

"You mean telling him you earned the money through sex with me?" Nico asks, and I laugh when I see Gabriel's eyes shoot towards me in the rearview mirror – humor dancing in them.

"Yes. Exactly." I stretch my neck up to whisper in his ear, "Besides, you know my pussy is worth it. And my mouth. More, actually. I would give you a reminder of both if we were alone right now, but I don't think you want your cousin to see or hear how much I love having your cock choke me and stretch me open."

Nico's hand resting on my thigh presses into me, and I smile and kiss his ear before going back to sitting normally.

I peek up at him after a minute and smile, loving that he's fighting with himself to gain control.

A little giggle spills out of me, which only has his eyes cutting to mine sharply.

"Is something wrong, Nico?" I ask innocently.

"No," he says gruffly, and I pucker my lips in a silent air kiss.

His eyes turn to slits and he leans down to whisper in my ear this time, "You'll pay for that, *piccante*."

"Gladly."

CHAPTER 30
Nico

I didn't know I could love someone the way I do Cassie. I thought I wasn't capable because I hadn't felt the need to spend more than a night with a single woman. It wasn't until a red-haired siren pulled me close and drowned me in her ocean eyes that I came to know what I was missing, and I've been drowning ever since.

Cassandra fucking Connelly is the air I need to survive, and without her, I know I'd be lost and adrift a dark sea with no chance of survival.

"Nico, what did you do?" Cassie asks right when she walks through the door. She must've seen my gift for her on her way inside and isn't happy about it.

I'm in the kitchen cooking dinner and she storms in with her hands on her hips. "Did you seriously buy me that car for a second time?"

"I did." I nod. "Here, try this." I hold out the wooden spoon in my hand for her to try the sauce I'm making.

She pops her mouth open and takes a taste of the end of the spoon. Her eyes widen. "Oh, Nico, that's good."

"Hopefully that won't be the only time you say that tonight."

She rolls her eyes and crosses her arms. "You're trying to distract me with sex, but it won't work. I'm mad at you."

"Is that a challenge? Because, baby, I know I can distract you with sex and you won't be mad at me for buying you another car." I grab her hips and pull her close, planting a kiss to her pouty lips. "If you want a different car, you can choose whatever you'd like, but you're getting a car."

"No, I like that one. It's really nice," she grumbles, like it's such an inconvenience to admit. I give her another kiss and she relaxes further. Her arms uncross and slide up and around my neck. "Thank you," she whispers against my lips.

"You're welcome, *piccante*." My lips brush against hers with my words, and I plant soft kisses all along her bottom lip, from left to right. "Now, I'm almost done with dinner. Open a bottle of wine and relax until it's ready."

"Thank you." She lifts up on her toes and fully wraps her arms around my neck, squeezing me in a tight hug.

She's the most precious thing I'll ever hold in my arms, and I reluctantly let her go when I hear my sauce bubbling and need to stir it.

After spending the rest of the weekend in the city, it wasn't until I realized I had to drive her back home for classes that it hit me we live in two different fucking cities. So, I packed another suitcase and told her I'd be staying with her until she graduates, and that I'll just travel back and forth for work when needed.

"How were your classes?"

She sighs. "Fine. I can't wait to be done."

"Me too. Then I can fuck you morning, noon, and night without worrying I'm too much of a distraction from your schoolwork."

I was only semi-joking, but Cassie bursts out laughing. A beautiful sound that has me staring at her with a smile on my face. Fuck, she's gorgeous.

"That'd be way too much, Nico." She chuckles, taking a sip of wine. "But I like where your head is at."

"My other head would like to be in the same place," I quip, throwing her a wink before turning the stove off and covering the saucepan.

"Nico!" she squeals all cute, laughing. "You know, you're really good at that. You can turn anything dirty, and I love it."

I swoop in and kiss the side of her neck with an onslaught of pecks until she's giggling and squirming away.

With the mess of her brother and the McLaughlins behind us, I just want to see her happy and free from the pressures of everything. I want to love her like she deserves.

"You're playful tonight," she says, smiling up at me.

"How could I not be? I've got everything I need right in front of me," I tell her, and she gasps in a short breath right before my lips meet hers, and I give her the slow, take my time to savor her, kiss that has her eyes hazy and filled with wonder. "Let me finish dinner."

Cassie gives me a small nod, and I go back to the stove to test if the pasta is soft yet. I drain it and take the meatballs from the oven.

I make the both of us a plate, and when I place one in front of Cassie, she smiles. "Spaghetti and meatballs. Isn't this a cliché meal for you to make me?" she teases, twirling her pasta around her fork.

"A little, but it's my nonna's recipe and I wanted you well fed and happy when I ask you something."

Her fork freezes midway to her mouth and she brings it back down to her plate. "What is it?"

"Nothing to panic about, *piccante*."

"Then don't phrase it like that. What is it?"

"I was wondering if you'd come to Sunday dinner with me next week to meet the rest of my family."

"Really?" she asks, a look I haven't seen in her eyes taking over.

"Yes, really. I want you to meet my mom. I know she'll love you. My sister, too. If you can go up against Stef with your death glare and mouth off to Leo, then you're golden, baby."

"Oh," she breathes, her cheeks staining pink like she's retroactively embarrassed for both. "Then I...I'd love to meet your family."

"And Lexi will be there too, I'm sure. So you'll have her."

She perks up immediately. "Okay. I can charm the shit out of everyone, don't worry."

"Not necessary. Just be yourself."

Her smile falls. "Are you saying my usual self isn't charming?"

"Fuck, I didn't mean that," I say quickly. "I meant, just be yourself. You don't have to try and be someone you think they'll like. You're enough. You're more than enough."

"Mmm," she huffs. "That's a better answer. Thank you."

Shaking my head, I smile and take a large sip of wine to occupy my mouth so I don't say anymore bullshit.

"Will the women your cousins are will be there too?"

"Yes. Everyone. Aunts, uncles, cousins, significant others. Even my cousins who are in Miami will fly back for it if they can. You'll be able to meet them before Sean goes down there. I'm glad he agreed to it."

Sean is staying in one of the empty apartments in our building in the city right now while he finishes healing up before he goes down to Miami.

We have a doctor on call if he needs it, and with how secure our building is, he won't be able to sneak out and no one can sneak in. That's what sold Cassie on him staying there for a couple weeks.

"Me too," she says. "Where do they live? Where will Sean be living?"

"They live in lofts above the club we own. Dance club," I quickly clarify when I see her eyes narrow. "It's a massive place, and we converted the upper part of the building into lofts. Sean will start off being their assistant, and then we'll see what happens."

"I'll want to check on him at some point. I'll want to see with my own eyes that he's doing well and going to meetings."

"So he agreed to go to Gambler's Anonymous?"

"He did. He doesn't want to be in that situation ever again. He knows how lucky he is that I was able to help him. And you, of course. You're the one who actually helped him."

"You're his sister, Cassie. *You* helped him."

"Thank you," she says softly, and pushes a meatball around her pasta.

"A trip to Miami means I get to see you in a bikini while the sun kisses your perfect skin. I'll have to religiously apply sunscreen all over you to make sure you don't burn. I hope you know that."

I wanted to lighten the mood again, and it worked. Her smile is instant, and she's rolling her pretty blue eyes at me.

"I'm lucky to have such a vigilant boyfriend."

"Boyfriend, huh?"

"Should I call you something else?"

"Not yet." I wink, and her cheeks heat. I fully plan on her calling me her husband within the year. I'd ask her to marry me now if I thought she'd say yes. "I've just never been someone's boyfriend before, so it's interesting to hear. And calling me a boy is a little insulting, no?"

"Do you want me to say manfriend instead?"

"That just sounds made up."

"Then what do you want?"

"Boyfriend will have to do for now."

"Yes, it will." Cassie pushes her hair over her shoulder in a haughty way that has me wanting to spank her perfect ass for being so sassy. But I fucking love it, and she knows it.

"These meatballs are amazing," she says, moaning around a bite. "Now that I'm in the family, do I get to know the recipe? I'd love to be able to make these for you next time."

I don't think she realizes what she just said and how much it means to me. She's admitting so casually that she's a part of the family now, and my heart fucking swells in my chest with pride and love. I want her to have the kind of family she's been denied her entire life. The kind of family she deserves. It's been just her brother and her against the world for too long, and I want her to always feel safe, welcome, and loved.

"It's in my head, so I'll have to write it down for you."

"Thank you."

"Or we could make them together, and you can see how it's done. A recipe only gives so much information."

"I'd like that." She smiles. "I didn't know you like cooking. I won't lie...I liked walking in here and seeing you in the kitchen. It was sexy as hell."

"Was it?"

"Oh, yes." She nods, taking a sip of wine. "Very."

"I'll make sure I'm cooking every time you come home, then. I always want to be sexy for you."

"Then all you have to do is be breathing. Because you're sexy all the time." She gives me a flirty little wink that makes my chest puff with an ego boost. "But cooking? Even more so."

"And if I said I bought you cookies and cream ice cream at the store for dessert? Will I be even sexier?"

"How did you…?"

"You ordered it from room service our first weekend together. You said it was your favorite."

"And you remembered," she says dreamily.

"Of course. I remember everything about you, *piccante*."

"Well then, it looks like I'll be having two desserts tonight." Cassie swirls more pasta around her fork and slides it into her mouth. Sauce leaks out onto the corners of her lips and she licks it away seductively, keeping her eyes on me.

My cock stiffens, wanting her tongue to circle around me like that.

"Is that so?"

"Mmhmm. I don't mind a little salty with my sweet."

Her eyes are dancing with mischief, and I push my plate away and turn my chair out to the side like I did for her not too many nights ago.

"Finished already?" she asks innocently, biting into the last meatball on her plate.

"Yes. I'm ready whenever you are."

Cassie laughs softly to herself. "I'm almost done."

"You should leave room. Two desserts can be filling."

"I can handle it."

Cassie finishes off the meatball and washes it down with the rest of the wine in her glass. She pours herself a little more from the bottle and leans back in her chair, her eyes on me as she drinks her wine slowly.

This woman is going to make me wait.

She's going to tease and torture me like this for the rest of my life.

I should get used to it.

As long as she knows turnabout is fair play. Not that I could ever deny her for too long.

Fuck, okay, so she wins. She always wins and will always win.

I guess I'm just a man at the mercy of a spicy redhead who lights my fucking world on fire.

Cassie finishes off her wine and delicately places the glass down on the table. Her lips turn up in a sly grin as she stands and takes the three steps around the table to me.

"Ice cream first?" she asks, planning on teasing me some more.

Growling, I grab her wrist and pull her towards me so she falls against my chest. "No."

"No?" Her eyebrows lift in surprise and I shake my head. "Hmm, if you insist." Cassie plants a soft kiss to my lips and slides down to her knees. "On second thought, maybe you shouldn't fill me up too much. I still want ice cream."

I pinch her chin. "You're going to swallow every drop of my come." Her eyes melt before me the way they do when I give her an order. "Understand?"

She gives me a lazy nod and I release her from my grip so she can get to work.

She's absolutely perfect.

And she's absolutely all mine.

CHAPTER 31

Cassie

5 months later...

"Hey, Cass, how was I out there? I tried the new move you taught me and I think I got it. Did it look okay?"

"Are you kidding me? You fucking killed it!" I tell Jamie excitedly. "You nailed the helicopter spin we were working on, too!"

"Yay!" She jumps and claps, and scurries off to her station in the dressing room. She's so adorable. She's only nineteen, and has these big brown eyes and a cute face that exude an air of innocence that the men here love.

She was my first hire at the Dark Horse club in New York, and I couldn't be prouder with how well she's doing.

When I told Nico I thought I'd be a good house mom, he was surprised I'd want to work at a strip club after everything that happened. But after I graduated, I was a little lost and unsure of what I wanted to do, so I started taking pole classes again for fun, and it got me thinking again about how I thought it'd be fun to be a house mom and foster a safe and fun environment for the women of the club.

I'm glad the Carfano clubs aren't like Pandemonium was. The moment a man becomes handsy, loud, aggressive, suggestive, or anything that makes the dancers uncomfortable, they're gone. Security is tight, and I always feel safe there. Of course, it helps that I'm Nico's girl, so everyone is respectful and constantly looking after me to make sure I'm good.

"Tanya, you're up in five with Jess, Eden, and Vivi," I read out from my clipboard. "Kylie, Sara, and Taylor, you're in the cages."

I love my job. These girls are amazing, and I always make sure they only do what they want. I even implemented a monthly wardrobe stipend so the girls can always have a fresh rotation of clothes and shoes that's not out of their own pocket. It's a win-win for them and the club if they're always looking new and fresh for every shift they work.

I'm younger than the typical house mom is, which usually goes to a retired dancer. But according to the girls, their last one was fine, but she only did the bare minimum for them by making the schedule. They said she always had an attitude and wasn't accommodating to any of their needs.

Nico had no problem firing her when he talked to the dancers to see their thoughts on bringing in someone new. I made him do that. I wasn't going to just swoop in and take over the job of someone that was liked by everyone already.

Nico was supportive of me taking this job, with his one request being that it was the day shift so I could be home with him every night. That, of course, was no problem for me. I don't want to work until the middle of the night and then always come home to find him asleep.

I check my phone and see a message from Nico that instantly makes me smile.

Nico: I miss you, *piccante*. When you get home, I have a surprise for you and I want you naked within thirty seconds.

Me: Or I could give you a little show first...

Me: I need to practice my routine for my next showcase, and I want your opinion on it.

Nico had a pole installed in his apartment for me, and it's been one of my favorite ways to get him riled up. He always fucks me like a dirty slut afterwards, and I fucking love it.

Nico: Fuck yeah, baby. Can you leave early?
Me: Nope.
Nico: With one phone call, I can have you fired so you have no choice but to come home.

Me: If you do that, I won't be coming home. Patience is rewarded, Nico.

Nico: It better be.

Smiling, I bite my lip.

I know he's pouting right now because he's not getting his way, which means he's going to be all the more savage later after making him wait.

But after an hour, it's me who can't stop thinking about going home early. I don't know how I'm going to make it another two hours.

I'm pacing the dressing room, talking myself in and out of leaving early, when all the girls come back in and start packing their stuff up.

"What's going on?"

"I don't know. We were told to get off stage and leave," Jess says, shrugging.

"Jon said we're closing for a few hours because someone smelled gas in the basement when they went to get a case of vodka for the bar."

Jon is the manager, but he hasn't sent me a message or anything about it, so I go and find him.

"What's happening, Jon?"

"We have to close for a couple hours."

"Someone smelled gas?"

He grins and shakes his head. "No, that's just a cover."

"Okay," I say, dragging out the word. "I don't understand."

"You will. I'll see you tomorrow, Cassie." He rounds up the bartenders and waitresses to leave, and I'm getting a flashback to a very similar occurrence from five months ago.

That's when I look around and see one man still here, sitting right in front of the main stage.

One man who is crazy enough to have a packed club emptied so he can have me all to himself.

"I'm waiting, Cassandra," Nico says, his head not even bothering to turn around to know that I'm here. "Don't keep me waiting too long."

I hurry back to the dressing room and go to the rack of brand-new outfits and accessories I keep stocked in here in case a girl needs something and forgot to bring it.

I choose the ice blue bodysuit that I've been dying to try on since I bought it. It has an eighties feel to it because it's a thong style that's high cut on the hips like a Baywatch bathing suit, and a deep 'v' in the front down to my pussy that laces up just far enough so my nipples are covered.

I take a pair of silver glitter pleaser heels from the rack and secure my feet in them before adding a little lipstick and fluffing my hair out.

The music is controlled from a system hooked-up to a laptop off stage, and I put on "Earned It" by The Weekend. I chose this song for my showcase coming up because I choreographed the routine with Nico in mind. He's always telling me I earned the fucking he gives me after every performance I give him at home. So now it's him who's earned this dance.

The Weekend's voice starts singing, and I wait for the first downbeat of the drums to saunter out onto stage. Nico's eyes immediately eat me up and he adjusts himself in the chair.

I knew he'd like this outfit.

This time is much different than the first. I give him a small smile and a wink, and get right into my routine – showing him everything he's earned these past five months.

When I end my performance crawling to him at the end of the stage, he stands in front of me and reaches for my hair, twirling a piece around his finger.

He tugs on it and I slide my hand around his neck to give him a kiss. "That was your best performance yet, *piccante*," he tells me, and I can feel his pulse pounding in his neck under my touch. "And I love this new outfit. But you're never wearing this outside of our home again. Your pussy swallowed the fabric every time you spread those sexy legs of yours, and I know it's soaked in your juices right now." He cups my pussy and bites my bottom lip. "Because I know how much dancing for me turns you on."

"Yes," I sigh, moving my hips against his hand.

"And I like this," he says, pulling the string in the front of the bodysuit so my boobs spill out. "Easy access for a taste."

Nico plants kisses all around my nipples until they're hard as pebbles before he flicks them with his tongue. I cry out – so sensitive.

"Nico," I moan, and he smiles against my chest.

"Just what I wanted," he murmurs right before he takes one of my nipples into his hot mouth and a bolt of lightning spikes through me and straight to my core.

"Nico," I moan again, and he does the same to my other nipple, making me whimper with the intensity.

I can feel my pulse in my clit, pounding for attention.

"Please, Nico," I beg.

"What do you need, *la mia rossa piccante*?"

"You know," I say, breathless.

He releases my nipple with a wet pop, and I moan, pulling myself closer to him.

"I do know." His hand cups my pussy again. "I know this greedy pussy needs attention."

"Yes," I hiss, rolling my hips against him.

"Let me feast before I fuck you, baby. Show me how wet you are for me." I lay back and spread my knees, and Nico groans. "Fuck."

He grabs me behind the knees and hooks them over his shoulders before he gets to work, sucking me right through the fabric.

He pulls the bodysuit to the side with his teeth and I shudder. I was already so wound up, it only takes a few passes of his tongue swirling around my clit before I'm shaking, ready to explode.

Nico doesn't let me come, though. He lifts his mouth away and I grunt, lifting my hips to chase him, but he just chuckles darkly. "Not yet, *piccante*."

"Nico," I growl, which only has him smiling like a hunter who's finally caught his prey.

"I want you to come on my cock, Cassandra."

"I can do both."

"Yes, but I have my reasons." Nico lifts me off the stage to stand in front of him, and then spins me around and presses between my shoulder blades so I'm bent at the waist, gripping the edge of the stage.

I look over my shoulder at him. "What reasons?"

"Just one. And you'll know soon enough," he teases, slapping my bare ass cheek.

I bite my lip and moan, pushing my hips back at him.

"That's my girl. So eager."

I hear the zipper of his pants fall and Nico nudges my feet apart. He hooks his finger under the fabric covering my pussy and pulls it to the side. The broad head of his cock teases me at my entrance, but he doesn't go any further.

I try and push back at him to do it myself, but he holds me in place.

"What are you doing?" I whine. "I need you to fuck me, Nico."

"I know, baby. But if you want that, then I need you to answer a question for me honestly."

Is he serious? Now? "Fine. Ask."

"Do you know how much I love you?" he asks, and I'm so caught off guard by the question, I don't answer right away, and he slaps my ass. "Have I not shown you how much all this time? Told you how much?" He slaps my ass again, and I can feel myself dripping onto his waiting cock.

"Yes!" I scream out.

"Good." He caresses where he slapped me, nudging his cock at my entrance. "And I know how much you love me."

"Yes," I moan, contracting my pussy over and over, trying to get him inside me.

"In that case, will you marry me?"

My heart constricts, and then takes off double-time. "What?"

"Marry me, Cassandra."

I turn my head and look over my shoulder to see how sincere his eyes are, and they penetrate me to my soul. He's serious.

"Is this really how you're asking me?"

"Yes. I had a whole thing set up at home, but you wouldn't leave early and I couldn't wait." He nudges just a little more against my entrance until he slips the tip in.

Ohmygod.

Moaning, I pinch my eyes closed. I'm feeling too much in every part of my body.

"I'm waiting for an answer, Cassandra. You give me the right answer and I'll fuck you so good, you'll feel it for days."

"Nico," I moan, my inner muscles flexing around him.

"That's not an answer."

"Yes," I whisper, but it's not good enough for him.

"I didn't hear that, Cassandra. Say it louder."

He starts to pull out, and I yell, "Yes! I'll marry you!"

"Alright then," he says smugly, and buries himself in me in a single thrust. "Fuck," he groans. "This is my pussy." I moan my agreement. "And this is your dick, baby." He pulls out and slams right back in. "For the rest of our lives."

I gasp, then moan, "Yes."

Nico fucks me so hard, I know I'll be sore in the most delicious way for days to come. He's laying claim to his future wife, and that thought alone has me ready to come harder than ever before.

"Come. Now," he commands, and my body already knows to listen because it *has* been trained by him.

I think I black out for a few seconds, because my ears are ringing and my eyes are blurry. But that's just from my screams and the emotions flooding out of me.

Nico growls behind me as he slides both his hands up my back and around to cup my breasts. He pinches my nipples, and I'm so far gone and spent, I cry out and collapse forward against the stage as another orgasm rips through me and Nico fills me with his come.

I didn't think I had anything left to give.

I lose all sense of time, direction, feeling, and consciousness, because the next thing I know, I'm being carried by two strong arms that feel like absolute heaven and safety around me.

"What took you so long to ask me?" I mumble against him, and he tugs on the ends of my hair.

"Should I have asked you after the first week like I wanted to?" he asks. I know he's kidding, but I answer him honestly.

"Maybe after the second or third week. I probably would've said yes then."

"Well, fuck me, *piccante*. I'm sorry I waited so long."

"You're forgiven." I yawn. I'm so tired. "And you can apologize again later by letting me actually come on your tongue this time."

"You're perfect," he says, the amazement in his voice warming my heart.

"I know."

He slaps my ass. "*La mia rossa piccante.*"

SONGS IN CAPTIVATED:

1. "Closer" by Nine Inch Nails – private dance in Dark Horse (AC)
2. "High" by Whethan and Dua Lipa – performance in Pandemonium
3. "Earned It" by The Weekend – private dance in Dark Horse (NYC)

SOME SONGS THAT INSPIRED ME WHILE WRITING AND GIVE NICO & CASSIE VIBES:
(in no particular order)

1. "Spicy" by Ty Dolla $ign ft. Post Malone
2. "Porn Star Dancing" by My Darkest Days ft. Ludacris
3. "Beautiful Things" by Benson Boone
4. "Woke Up In Love" by Kygo, Gryffin, & Calum Scott
5. "The Archer" by Taylor Swift
6. Guilty as Sin?" by Taylor Swift
7. "Lately" by Caitlyn Smith
8. "The Way" by Kehlani ft. Chance The Rapper
9. "Control" by Bryce Savage
10. "Easy to Love" by Bryce Savage
11. "The High" by Bryce Savage
12. "Daydreams" by We Three
13. "Kiss Me" by Ed Sheeran
14. "Dive" by Ed Sheeran
15. "Intrusive Thoughts" by Natalie Jane

ACKNOWLEDGMENTS

Thank you to each and every reader who has read my books! If I didn't have you, then I'd be nowhere! Knowing you're looking forward to the next in the series is always what keeps me going, and keeps me driven.

Love you all!!

ABOUT THE AUTHOR

Rebecca is a dreamer through and through with permanent wanderlust. She has an endless list of places to go and see, hoping to one day experience the world and all it has to offer.

She's a Jersey girl who dreams of living in a place with freezing cold winters and lots of snow! When she's not writing, you can find her planning her next road trip and drinking copious amounts of coffee (preferably iced!).

newsletter, contact me, blog, shop, & links to all social medias:
www.rebeccagannon.com

Follow me on Instagram to stay up-to-date on new releases, sales, teasers, giveaways, and so much more!
@rebeccagannon_author

Printed in Dunstable, United Kingdom